The room went silent.

A shiver ran up Kara's spine and suddenly she was struck by a strange feeling of dread. The carefully blank expression on Mike's face as he put down the telephone did nothing to dispel it.

'He's not going to make it in time for the wedding, is he? What's his excuse?' she demanded in a resigned tone.

It wasn't so much that she minded missing out on the reception. What she did regret was the fact that it looked as if Mac was going to arrive too late for them to get married today.

Josie Metcalfe lives in Cornwall now with her long-suffering husband, four children and two horses, but, as an army brat frequently on the move, books became the only friends who came with her wherever she went. Now that she writes them herself she is making new friends, and hates saying goodbye at the end of a book—but there are always more characters in her head clamouring for attention until she can't wait to tell their stories.

Recent titles by the same author:

TAKE TWO BABIES...
A TRUSTWORTHY MAN
BE MY MUMMY
INSTANT FATHER CHRISTMAS

A MILLENNIUM MIRACLE

BY
JOSIE METCALFE

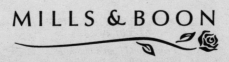

MILLS & BOON

With grateful thanks to FRC and BTM for attempting to
simplify the immense complexities of neurology for me.
Any errors in comprehension are obviously mine.

*First published in Great Britain 1999
Harlequin Mills & Boon Limited,
Eton House, 18-24 Paradise Road, Richmond, Surrey TW9 1SR*

© Josie Metcalfe 1999

ISBN 0 263 81916 7

*Set in Times Roman 10½ on 12 pt.
03-0001-49368*

*Printed and bound in Spain
by Litografia Rosés S.A., Barcelona*

CHAPTER ONE

SHE'D tell him tonight.

Kara felt a smile creep over her face as she smoothed her hands over the heavy ivory fabric of her dress, imagining Mac's reaction to the news.

'I know what *that* smile's for. You're thinking wicked thoughts already,' muttered a laughing voice beside her under the cover of the gentle murmur of conversation surrounding them. 'Wait a couple of hours, please, or you'll make the rest of us jealous!'

Kara turned with a soft chuckle to face her friend, seated on the seat beside her in the anteroom. She and Sue Leonard had met on their first day in Obs and Gyn at St Augustine's Hospital and had been firm friends ever since.

Even Sue's non-stop teasing about the fact that she herself had met Mac at the same time, and had instantly lost her heart to him, hadn't affected their friendship. With all three of them working full-time shifts, there was always someone just going to work or just leaving.

Anyway, Mac wasn't the obsessive sort. He was quite happy for Kara to have her own circle of friends and got on well with them when they all socialised as a group.

As she did with Mac's friends, especially Mike, their best man today.

Today. Her wedding day.

Her heart gave a quick flip of a double somersault

inside her chest when she contemplated the fact that, in a matter of minutes, she and Mac would be married.

They had both been happy with their situation before—both working full time and spending all their free time with each other even before they'd moved into their tiny flat together.

She was fulfilling her ambition of working in a busy obstetrics and gynaecology department while Mac was steadily progressing towards a consultancy in neurology and neurosurgery.

Neither of them had been in any hurry to get married, but suddenly the time had seemed right.

It had been Sue who had insisted that Kara and Mac couldn't possibly slope off to the registry office for an anonymous little ceremony. She had been the one to badger them into inviting just a handful of their closest friends to the ceremony and then to a small reception at a local hotel afterwards.

Kara was certain that it had been Sue who had prompted Mac into insisting that she bought something special to wear, otherwise she wouldn't have dreamed of having such a beautiful dress. She hadn't a doubt, though, that Mac would have arranged the delivery of the same beautiful bouquet—he was thoughtful that way.

Kara smiled mischievously. 'Can I help it if I'm happy to be marrying the sexiest man in the known universe?' she whispered.

'Please!' Sue groaned and rolled her eyes, but Kara didn't care. Meeting Mac, it had been the best thing that had ever happened in her life and she didn't mind who knew it.

'There's the wedding ceremony and the reception

to get through first,' Sue reminded her. 'I'm warning you now, I shall be giving the two of you a swift dig in the ribs if you start staring into each other's eyes and forgetting the rest of us are around. No one would believe you've already been living together for a year.'

One year, two months and eleven days, Kara corrected silently. She'd actually added it up when she and Mac had settled on today for their wedding, surprised how short it really was when it seemed as if she'd known him all her life.

'We'll behave!' she promised with a grin. 'At least, *I* will.'

'Anyway,' Sue continued slightly sheepishly, apparently avoiding meeting Kara's eyes by smoothing imaginary creases out of her new figured silk dress, 'while Mike's out checking up on whether Mac's arrived, I want to know how come you haven't introduced the two of us before. So far, all I know about him is that he and Mac are long-time friends.'

'I don't know how you haven't met him at some stage over the last year or so. He's been down to visit a couple of times. Now, what do you want to know…and why?' Kara teased.

She couldn't help having noticed that Sue had been impressed with Mike as soon as they'd met, or that the attraction seemed to be reciprocated. It was certainly more than the fact that they were well matched physically, both tall, blond and athletic-looking with outgoing personalities.

Having made her wait, Kara took pity on Sue by supplying a potted history. 'They met at medical school and found they worked well together. Then both decided to specialise in neurology and neurosurgery. Obviously, they work at different hospitals now, but they've made the effort to keep in touch. Apparently, when he heard, Mike teased Mac about being committed to an institution—the institution of marriage—but he was delighted to be asked to stand as best man.'

She couldn't help glancing at the watch Mac had given her last Christmas, checking that it showed the same time as the old schoolroom clock on the waiting-room wall. 'I wonder how much longer it'll be before Mac arrives. It's only five minutes until it's our turn.'

'That's a point. It's traditional for the *bride* to arrive a few minutes late, not the groom,' Sue pointed out as she craned her neck to see if she could catch another glimpse of Mike. 'I thought it was part of the best man's job to get the groom here on time.'

Out of the corner of her eye Kara saw the registrar come in through the other door, a very smart older woman wearing the sort of dress and coat ensemble that wouldn't have looked out of place on the mother of the bride.

Obviously, the ceremony for her previous clients had finished and she was ready for them now.

Kara saw her looking at her watch, too, the movement picked up by several members of the small group of friends and colleagues gathered in the anteroom, waiting to go through for the ceremony.

Mike came back into the room but there was no sign of Mac following him in.

'Well, he's officially late now,' Kara pointed out when Mike joined them, significantly choosing to sit on the other side of Sue.

'Of course he's late! That's what you get for agreeing to marry a doctor!' teased Mike, his blue eyes made even bluer by the semi-permanent tan of an outdoor sport fanatic. He winked at Sue. 'He's obviously starting as he means to go on.'

Kara watched the byplay in a detached sort of way. She and Mac had laughed at the fact that they were hoping that their friends would be attracted to each other during the course of the celebrations.

But the celebrations couldn't even get started until he arrived.

Surreptitiously, she smoothed her hand over her skirt again under the cover of the spray of ivory-coloured freesias that Mac knew were her favourites, relishing her secret just a little bit longer.

The two of them hadn't actually intended starting a family straight away, but they were both fully qualified and had good jobs and both of them had long ago agreed that they wanted at least two children. It was just happening a little sooner than they'd expected.

Not that Mac should be too surprised, the way passion flared between them at the slightest opportunity. It was more of a surprise that it hadn't happened the very first time desire had overtaken them, rather than as the result of a course of antibiotics prescribed by her dentist.

As medical professionals, they should have known better than to have trusted her pills to work under those circumstances, but it had coincided with that magical trip...

She remembered her excitement when Mac had met her from work with bags already packed and tickets for a surprise weekend in Paris.

He'd waited until they'd reached the end of their

meal that evening, within sight of the Eiffel Tower, before he'd formally proposed, presenting her with the delicate antique diamond ring that had once belonged to his grandmother.

A phone rang at the far side of the anteroom, startling Kara out of her happy reminiscing. She watched the registrar reach out to answer it. After the barest minimum of conversation she covered the mouthpiece over with her other hand and looked up.

'Which one of you is Dr Prowse?'

Almost before the woman stopped speaking, Mike was on his feet.

The room went silent and all eyes were on him as he responded to the call with frustratingly brief monosyllables.

'Yes, I'm Mike Prowse. Who...?' Kara watched his eyebrows draw together, frustrated that she wasn't close enough to hear what was being said. She just knew that it was something about Mac.

A shiver ran up her spine and suddenly she was struck by a strange feeling of dread. The carefully blank expression on Mike's face did nothing to dispel it as he broke the connection.

'He's not going to make it in time for the wedding, is he? What's his excuse?' she demanded in a resigned tone, hearing their guests murmuring their speculations.

It wasn't so much that she minded missing out on the reception—she'd never been concerned about making any sort of splash so it wouldn't matter to her if it didn't happen.

What she did regret was the fact that it looked as if Mac was going to arrive too late for them to get married today.

'Kara, that was the accident and emergency department at St Augustine's. There's been an accident,' Mike began softly.

'And Mac being Mac, even though he's not on duty, has gone in to do a neurological assessment on one of the victims, forgetting that we're all here waiting for him?' she suggested.

A similar thing had happened once before, soon after they'd met, when he'd become so involved in an accident case that he'd completely forgotten he'd left her waiting in a cinema foyer.

'How late is he going to be? Will we have to make another appointment here?'

'Kara…' Mike bent forward to capture both of her hands in his and there was no sign of his teasing smile. Suddenly, the steely tension in his hands communicated itself to her, and she found herself jerking to her feet in fear.

A tiny corner of her mind registered that her beautiful bouquet had fallen onto the floor, where several fragile blossoms had broken off, but it was the pain in Mike's eyes that filled her with dread.

'Kara, it's *Mac* who's been in an accident. *He's* the one who's hurt.'

'No!' Shock and disbelief had her staring blankly at him, shaking her head as she tried to make sense of his words. 'No, Mike. Not Mac. Not Mac.'

A strange, hollow numbness surrounded her as he and Sue led her out of the building and settled her in Mike's car for the brief journey.

They were held up for a couple of minutes by snarled traffic at a crossroads where a white delivery van was being cut away from a scarlet Morgan so they could be towed away from the scene of the collision.

Kara stared at the grim sight, the medically trained side of her mind cataloguing what she was seeing and the likely effects it would have had on the humans involved.

Whoever had been driving that little car wouldn't have stood much chance of survival, not with the white van virtually ploughing its way through the smaller vehicle.

Sue and Mike might have spoken to her, but all she could hear were her own thoughts travelling round and round inside her head in a continuous loop.

Not for a moment while she'd sat in that little room, waiting for him, had she worried that Mac wouldn't turn up at the registry office…that he might have changed his mind and run out on her. There had been no doubt in either of their minds that they were doing the right thing. From the first moment they'd met, less than a year and a half ago, they'd both known that their marriage was as inevitable as…as daylight arriving the next day.

Except the world had turned topsy-turvy now, with no difference between day and night, as she travelled towards the hospital in her wedding finery to find out whether the man she loved—the father of her unborn baby—was going to live.

'Why do these rooms always look so barren…so grim?' Kara muttered distractedly.

Yet another set of feet approached the door and walked on by without stopping, but her pulse had hit the stratosphere in the meantime.

'It's not the room so much as the atmosphere in it,'

Sue whispered, her hand coming out to rest gently on Kara's clenched fist. 'Shall I see if I can find out anything new?'

'There's no point,' Kara said quietly. 'They'll come and tell me if he's…when there's something…' She shook her head, unable to finish.

She had to find something else to think about or she would go mad by the time she heard anything. The urge to scream and rage was growing all the time and was going to need a focus soon.

In the meantime, she needed to know how this terrible thing had come about.

'Mike, please, if Mac wasn't seeing a patient, what *was* he doing? I thought the two of you were supposed to be travelling to the ceremony together?'

'We did set off together, but he wanted me to drop him off at the garage on the way here to pick up the car he'd ordered.' Mike grimaced. 'He put his name down for it a long while ago. It's a wonderful little hand-built car and there's a waiting list of people wanting to buy. Apparently, he'd all but forgotten about it when suddenly he had notification that it was going to be ready just in time for today.'

He drew an unsteady hand through ruffled blond hair that had been continuously raked over the last few hours.

'He swore me to secrecy about it, but he wanted the two of you to go away in something a bit special.'

'We could always have picked the car up later,' Kara pointed out, trying desperately to rationalise something that could never be changed. Her fingers returned to their newly acquired habit of pleating the fabric of her dress until Sue stilled their action with a gentle touch.

'He said he wanted to have the surprise waiting outside the registry office so you could travel to the reception in it,' Mike explained. 'Anyway, he was going to lock all your cases in the boot of the car so no one could get at them with rice and confetti before you went away.'

That was typical of Mac. Always looking ahead and planning things so that they would run smoothly.

Except today something had gone disastrously wrong with his timing.

'What sort of car was it?' she asked, not really caring, but for the sake of her sanity she needed to talk about *something*.

'A Morgan,' Mike said quietly—almost reluctantly. 'He's had a thing about Morgans for years and—'

Kara gasped, her eyes widening in shock before she turned her head away sharply. She'd suddenly remembered seeing a little red Morgan earlier today. It had looked almost like a mangled child's toy under the big white van.

That must have been the car Mac had been driving. *That* must have been where he'd been injured.

Oh, God, she could remember thinking that no one could possibly survive such a crash...

But this was Mac, the man she loved. Mac couldn't have died in that crash, not before they'd been married—not before she'd had a chance to tell him about the baby they'd made...

All three of them turned towards the door when a slower, heavier set of feet approached, announcing the arrival of Professor Squires.

Kara had been certain she would know from the professor's face what had happened, but he'd had too many years of dealing with tragedy to allow anything to show.

'Professor?' Mike drew his attention, the single word a question in itself.

'He's on life support,' the eminent man said, those few brief words enough to tell Kara that Mac was still alive.

She dragged in a shaky breath and watched impatiently while he massaged the back of his neck with one hand, as though the muscles were knotted by stress. As usual, his schedule had been too busy for him to take time off to attend the wedding—a situation that had actually meant he'd been on hand to take care of Mac when he'd arrived at the hospital's emergency department.

'He had a catalogue of injuries when he was brought in—broken ribs, a broken arm, a large gash on his head, a broken nose…' He shook his head and sighed. 'When we scanned him we found a marked area of damage to the right side of his brain from the impact. He's been heavily sedated to minimise brain swelling so it could be some days before we have any conclusive results.'

Kara suddenly found her voice to ask the only important question. 'But he *is* going to be all right? He's not going to die?'

There was an achingly long silence while the professor seemed to choose his words carefully.

'My dear, for a young man, Darroch MacGregor was an excellent neurologist and a very gifted and promising neurosurgeon. He was an asset to the department and I valued him highly. Having said that, I sometimes feel that merely staying alive is not the best outcome. It might be as well to prepare yourself for the possibility that he might not—'

'No!' A mixture of fear, anger and passion drove her to her feet, although she was shaking so badly she didn't know how long it would be before she crumpled into a heap at his feet. 'Mac *will* recover. He loves us too much to leave us.'

Subconsciously, her hand flattened over her waist. There was nothing to show that she was pregnant yet, and she hadn't even had time to tell Mac, but *she* knew their child was there and she knew that as soon as he was well enough to be told Mac would be delighted too.

Professor Squire's sharp eyes had picked up the betraying gesture and he sighed heavily. 'Well, my dear, for your sake, I hope you're right.' He turned to walk away.

'Please?' Kara called him back. 'When can I go to him? I want… I *need* to be with him.'

'You're a nurse here, aren't you?' He half turned, displaying the start of middle-aged spread around his impressive figure as he gazed intently at her for a moment. He gave a single nod. 'As long as you don't disrupt my department I'll make sure you can visit whenever you're free.'

He disappeared from view before she could voice her thanks, his heavy steps receding like strange punctuation marks.

'Take your time. Mike and I will wait here for you,' Sue suggested when Kara began to hurry across the despised waiting room towards the open doorway.

'No. Please. Both of you, come with me.' She turned and addressed Mike directly. 'I need you to tell me what it all means. The machinery, Mac's case notes. I want you to have a look at him for me, too, to see if there's—'

'No,' Mike interrupted swiftly. 'Kara, I can't do that. It's against professional etiquette. You would have to inform the professor that you wanted a second opinion.'

'But I need to *know*,' she wailed, hovering between fierce determination and tears of desperation. 'I know so little about neurology when it gets to this level. And this is Mac, your friend.'

Mike sighed, obviously torn.

'I'll come with you and see what we can find out,' he promised, putting one arm around her shoulders and ushering her out into the corridor. 'Even if I have to use my charm on his nurse...'

During her training, Kara had done a spell on Accident and Emergency and had thought herself hardened to gruesome sights.

Nothing could have prepared her for her first sight of Mac when they entered the intensive care unit.

It was an enormous room, with individual cubicles along each side and a central station monitoring all the beds from the middle of the room.

With all that going on, it shouldn't have been possible for her eyes to pick Mac out immediately, but to her it was as if he was the only patient in the room.

'Oh, God,' she breathed, the word as fervent as any prayer. 'Oh, Mac.'

Oblivious of the senior sister's beckoning hand, she made her way towards him, feeling strangely like a sleepwalker. It almost seemed to take hours before she covered the few yards to his bedside, but every second her eyes were frantically scanning what she could see of him.

Professor Squires had obviously tried to warn her about his injuries, but her brain hadn't made the right connections. She just hadn't realised how *ill* he would look, how battered and bruised.

He'd said that Mac's arm was broken, and some ribs, but she hadn't registered the fact that it would mean strapping and bandages and a cast. Under this light, they looked almost luminously white against the soft olive tone of Mac's skin, while the darkening bruises looked livid.

The professor had mentioned the gash on Mac's head, but she'd never dreamed that so much of his hair, as dark as a moonless midnight, would have had to have been shaved away to facilitate the stitching. She wouldn't allow herself to think about any other explorations that might have been necessary before his skull had been covered again.

The damage from the broken nose looked as if it had given him two black eyes, but even that looked as if it had been carefully supported and taped into position.

'Perhaps they've even managed to straighten it for you,' Kara whispered with a wobbly smile, remembering the tale he'd told her of the rugby match that had put a kink in it long before she'd met him.

Except there was no answering smile from Mac. No signal that he'd even heard her over the soft cacophony of the complex monitoring equipment sustaining his life.

'Would you like a chair?' asked a soft voice. Kara blinked and turned towards it, finding the nurse who was apparently specialling Mac ushering her towards a seat next to the bed.

Her eyes were full of compassion but all Kara could manage was a nod of agreement as she half slid, half collapsed onto the chair and reached through the safety bars to wrap Mac's hand between hers.

Silently, she watched as the young woman entered the next set of observations onto Mac's case notes, and a sense of frustration started to grow.

He seemed to be surrounded by tubes and wires, almost as if he were tethered to the bed by them, like restraints on a wild animal. She could see that he had the usual leads attached to his chest to monitor his heartbeat and tubes running in and out of his body, delivering fluids or medication as required or removing urine.

She didn't like to think about his condition when he'd arrived in the emergency department, a condition that had forced the doctor to perform a cricothyrotomy rather than a simple intubation to maintain his breathing. Perhaps they'd originally thought he'd sustained much more damage to his face than just the broken nose.

He was surrounded by high-tech electronic displays, and in most cases she could even read the figures on them, but what did they all mean as far as Mac was concerned? As far as his recovery was concerned?

Her gaze must have been burning a hole in the clipboard because the young woman looked up and smiled.

'How much have you been told about his condition?' she asked softly, apparently quite willing to talk.

'Professor Squires said he's got various breaks and stitches and that the impact injured his brain so he has to be deeply sedated.'

'How much do you know about the sort of sedation we have to use for brain injuries?'

'A lot,' Mike replied for her as he arrived behind Kara and put one hand on her shoulder. 'I'm Mike Prowse, neurologist. Mac and I trained together.'

Kara saw the young woman's eyes widen as they went from the single rose still nestled in the button-hole of Mike's charcoal suit to the distinctive colour of her own dress.

'And you were…?' She gestured wordlessly be-tween Kara and Mike. 'What a thing to happen on your wedding day.'

'No,' Kara choked. 'It was *Mac* and I who were getting married.'

'Oh, God, I'm sorry. Then you must be Kara,' the young woman breathed. 'Mac often mentioned you. You work over on Obs and Gyn, don't you? But he hadn't said anything about…' She gestured again to-wards Kara's dress. 'If there's anything I can tell you, anything I can explain…'

'It's just so bloody ironic,' Mike said suddenly, 'for Mac to end up a patient in his own department.' He looked as if he wanted to hit something—hard.

'At least it means you know we'll take good care of him,' the young woman said. 'There will be six of us in the team, looking after him in shifts, and we all think the world of him. I'm Alison and I'm on with Gaynor today. You'll meet the others as the shifts change.'

'How much can you tell us?' Kara pleaded, glad to know that Mac's nurses thought well of him but desperate for more details. 'How much are you *allowed* to tell us?'

Alison's eyes strayed briefly towards Sue, standing just beyond the foot of the bed.

Kara forced a smile as she interpreted the slightly wary look. 'Sue's medical, too. She works with me over on Obs and Gyn.'

Alison beckoned Sue closer. 'If I go through it once, then—is it Mike? He can pick up on any of the technicalities I've missed,' she suggested.

'Starting with the simple things, his arm was a straightforward break—unfortunate, but no complications expected. Four of his ribs were broken. No perforation of the lung evident, but we're keeping an eye open for breathing complications. The scalp wound isn't pretty but it's relatively unimportant.'

She looked from Kara at one end of the bed to Sue at the other and received nods from both of them.

'Now we come to the grim part,' she warned. 'His major injury was a severe blow to the right side of his head. On admission, his GCS was only six.'

Kara's heart clenched inside her. Alison's shorthand referred to the Glasgow coma scale, which was used to give a rough indication of the severity of a brain injury.

A score of three to five indicated potentially fatal damage, especially if accompanied by fixed pupils or absent oculovestibular responses. Only a score of eight or above correlated with a high chance of good recovery.

'What about his signs and symptoms?' Mike prompted, almost as if he'd read Kara's mind.

'His pupils are fixed…no reaction to light. His corneal reflexes are down and there were no oculovestibular responses. His pulse rate is up, with signs of arrhythmia, and his blood pressure is different in each arm.'

Mike wasn't quite quick enough to hide his immediate response to that catalogue of horror and Kara felt sick.

'Pupils dilated?' he fired back at Alison over his shoulder as he stood looking down at his friend. 'What about stiff neck?'

'Yes to the pupils but I don't know about the neck. The X-rays were clear so the collar could come off, but while he's so heavily sedated we can't test for stiffness.'

'So there's third nerve compression but nothing conclusive to indicate or rule out inflammation of the brain stem,' Mike muttered, his eyes very intent on Mac's face.

Kara's eyes had been travelling backwards and forwards, like a spectator at a tennis match, but in her case there were three people to watch—Alison, Mike and Mac.

She realised that Mac's injuries were serious—she didn't need Mike's tension or his frown to tell her that. She also knew that such a set of findings could very well be a sentence of death for Mac, if not a living death in a permanent vegetative state.

Suddenly, all the confusion and dread that had been whirling around inside her own brain drained away, leaving her thoughts crystal clear.

Although she couldn't bear to lose Mac, neither would she want to condemn him to the hopeless indignity of mere survival.

But that wasn't going to happen—not if she had anything to do with it.

Deep inside, she was absolutely determined that she wasn't going to lose Mac, that he was going to survive this to come back to her and the child she was carrying.

If there was anything she could do to help the process along then she would do it. The only thing she didn't know was how long it was going to take.

CHAPTER TWO

DARKNESS...

Everywhere was dark. Everywhere...

Can't breathe... Can't move... Can't fight the darkness... Too tired to fight. Much easier just to...let go and drift...into the darkness...

'Kara, it's time you went home,' Sue said gently as she shook her friend's shoulder, her voice barely registering in Kara's tired brain. 'You haven't left the hospital for nearly three days.'

'No. I can't leave him,' Kara muttered, tightening her grip on Mac's hand. 'I've got to be here when he wakes up.'

She groaned when she tried to straighten up.

Heaven only knew how long ago it was since she'd dozed off with her back and neck bent at such uncomfortable angles.

Ita and Joanne had been on duty earlier, but now Alison was here again so she must have slept for several hours...

Her eyes flew towards Mac, urgently scanning his face the way she always did in case he'd woken up while she'd been asleep.

His eyelashes still spread out in thick, dark fans, more visible now that the bruising from his broken nose was beginning to fade into a rainbow of hues.

In spite of the fact that the machine was still breathing for him through the artificial hole in his throat, his lips were slightly parted, almost as though he had fallen asleep beside her in their bed and it would take only a kiss to wake him.

She dragged her eyes away and focused on each of the monitors in turn.

In three days she'd had time to learn what story each one of them told and her glance was almost as knowledgeable as that of one of her intensive care colleagues.

One half of her was disappointed that there seemed to have been no change in his condition, but the more optimistic side was quick to point out that it proved he hadn't grown any worse.

'Please, Kara,' Sue said, and grasped her wrist gently to draw her round. 'We're worried.'

'You don't have to worry about me,' Kara said quietly, bolstered by a resurgence of the determination she hadn't known she possessed until Mac had been so badly injured. 'I'll be all right.'

'But will you?' Alison demanded softly, coming over to join Sue at her side. 'There isn't just *you* to worry about, is there?' She glanced meaningfully towards Kara's waist, reminding her that the long, silent hours had given birth to many confidences. 'You can't afford to let yourself become exhausted.'

'Apart from that, you're going to need to be strong for Mac too,' Sue pointed out. 'With the best will in the world, he's going to need help when he comes out of the coma, even if it's only coping with a broken arm. Can you imagine how difficult it will be to pull up trousers zips with only one hand? He could end up doing himself a permanent injury.'

Kara couldn't help giggling at the picture that leapt into her tired mind.

'OK,' she conceded, only then realising just how many hours it had been since she'd first entered the department.

Her wedding dress had been exchanged for a pair of blue surgical scrubs, courtesy of Alison, and some time in the second long night she'd remembered to unpin the dying flowers Sue had woven into a small coronet in her hair.

They'd been freesias, 'stolen' from the bouquet that had been sent by Mac just before she and Sue had left for the registry office.

She had a sudden mental image of the bouquet hitting the floor when she'd stood up, shocked by the news of Mac's accident. In her mind she could see the fragile blossoms which had been snapped off on impact and she suddenly realised how symbolic it had been.

'We can keep each other company while we eat, and then you can doss down in my room for some sleep while I go on duty,' Sue said briskly, as she stood aside for Kara to leave Mac's bedside.

'Oh, but—I hadn't intended staying away very long,' Kara began.

One look at the determination in the matching expressions on Sue's and Alison's faces told her she may as well give in now. They obviously weren't going to let her win this argument.

'OK. But I'm coming back as soon as I wake up,' she insisted.

'Agreed,' Alison said with a touch of relief in her voice. 'I'll even make you a cup of tea if I'm still on duty.'

Kara leaned forward to stroke Mac's face, feeling the new growth of his beard roughening his skin.

She'd had her first lesson in shaving a comatose patient this morning, utterly relieved that she'd been allowed to do something for him. It was so hard just to sit there, feeling helpless. It left far too much time for remembering the past and dreading how different the future they'd planned might be.

'Bye for now, my love,' she whispered as she leaned forward to press a kiss to the corner of Mac's lips. 'I'll be back soon.'

She gave his hand one last squeeze before she reluctantly let go.

It was strange to realise that while she had been concentrating on willing Mac to return to consciousness life had been continuing as usual all around her.

While she and Sue made their way towards the staff canteen, people were bustling in every direction. After several days of staying almost completely still, she felt quite disorientated, and was glad when they reached their destination and found an empty table near a corner.

Sue hurried off and Kara knew that she was probably going to fetch a selection of foods again. Pregnancy might have been affecting her appetite slightly, but she'd hardly been able to face eating any food, knowing that Mac lay helpless. That, however, hadn't stopped Sue from trying to tempt her with imaginative choices.

'You are actually going to eat some of this food,' Sue announced firmly as she slid a laden tray onto the table.

'Good Lord, how many are you feeding?' Kara exclaimed with a startled laugh. 'There must be seven different dishes there.'

'Well, blame that on Rhoda, behind the counter,'

Sue said with a grin. 'She decided you were going to have a little of each to see which one took your fancy.'

Kara had been reaching for a small plate with a serving of macaroni cheese, the topping all crispy and golden brown, when her hand froze in mid-air.

Her eyes flew to Sue's, full of silent questions.

Sue didn't pretend to misunderstand.

'You know what the hospital grapevine is like,' she said with a shrug. 'I don't suppose there's anyone who doesn't know what's happened, including the taxi drivers in the stand by the front entrance.'

'And all this...' Kara gestured towards the selection of meals.

'It's probably just Rhoda's way of saying she's thinking of you. She certainly wouldn't let me pay for any of it.'

Kara felt the quick sting of tears and was surprised. So far she hadn't cried at all—hadn't dared let herself cry because the magnitude of her fear and sorrow were too large to bear.

How strange that a simple kindness by someone who prided herself on being almost invisible as she went about her daily work should mean so much.

She drew in a deep breath and took the plate off the tray, setting it down in front of her with a definite air of decision.

Deliberately, she looked across at the serving counters and met the worried gaze of the slender woman behind them. She almost seemed to have been waiting for her to look up.

'Thank you,' Kara mouthed silently and lifted her hand in acknowledgement.

Rhoda's answering smile seemed almost shy and

she immediately broke eye contact and hurried to start serving the next person standing in front of her.

In spite of her preoccupation, or perhaps because of it, Kara finished the serving of macaroni cheese and tasted at least a couple of forkfuls of each of the other two savoury dishes.

Having become unaccustomed to eating over the last few days, she didn't think she could possibly manage another thing, but when Sue slid a small dish of fresh fruit salad in front of her, it was far too easy to nibble at it. Especially when her devious friend distracted her with questions about Mike.

Mac's friend had only been able to visit once since the accident and that had been on the day immediately following it. Then he'd had to return to work, but had promised he was only on the other end of a phone line if Kara needed him.

The last thing he'd done before he'd left had been to take her to one side and hand her a familiar velvet-covered box.

'Mac had already given this to me, ready for the ceremony,' he'd explained softly as he'd pressed it into her trembling hand.

Dimly, Kara had realised that she hadn't even wondered what had happened to their wedding rings, and then there they'd been in her hand, both nestled together in white satin, one completely inside the other because her fingers were so slender.

She'd tightened her hand around the box as she'd thanked Mike, suddenly feeling as if she'd been handed a talisman.

The two rings were the outward symbol of their love for each other and she was going to keep them close to her heart until Mac was well enough for them to be transferred to the places they belonged.

It hadn't taken long for their weight on a thin chain around her neck to become familiar, and she'd quickly developed a habit of rubbing them with her fingers.

She was toying with them now, feeling much more mellow after her first real food and conversation in days.

Sue cleared her throat suddenly and Kara tightened her fingers around the rings, realising that there was some serious conversation coming.

'Kara, Sister Harris needs to know when you're coming back to work—or if you're coming back,' Sue said quietly. 'Obs and Gyn can cope with scheduled holidays and suchlike, but she'd have to replace you if you took indefinite leave.'

'I can't come back,' Kara declared instantly, trying to imagine how she could possibly keep her mind on her job when Mac needed her so much. He was still totally dependent on the ventilator to keep him alive while they waited for a brain scan to show evidence that the swelling was going down.

'But, Kara, what are you going to do for money?'

'Sue…! It's only been a couple of days. Mac and I were going to take a long weekend off after the wedding—'

'Kara,' Sue broke in sharply. 'You were supposed to be returning to work tomorrow. It will have been four days…'

'Four!' Kara was stunned. Had she really been by Mac's side that long? Time didn't seem to mean anything any more.

'You know we're all praying that Mac comes out

of the coma soon, but—don't kill me for saying it—
what happens if he doesn't?' her friend demanded,
her hazel eyes full of compassion.

'He will,' Kara insisted fiercely, unable to bear
thinking about the alternative. 'Dammit, Sue, he *will*
come out of it. He has to.'

'OK, Kara. OK.' Sue covered Kara's clenched fist
with a gentle hand. 'But what if it takes time? You
know you're pregnant and you're going to need your
job if you're going to support the baby as well as
yourself. And what if Mac needs a long spell of rehab
before he's fit to start working again?'

Kara released a shuddering sigh then drew in another deep breath.

'You're right, Sue,' she admitted wearily, her
shoulders slumping. 'And I'm sorry for jumping
down your throat. It's just… Mac's sedation will
gradually be reduced as soon as the swelling in his
brain starts subsiding. He could start coming out of
the coma any day now.'

'And, understandably, you want to be there when
it happens,' Sue finished for her. She piled the last of
their used utensils back on the tray and made to get
up.

'Look,' she said, sinking back into her seat again,
'can I make a suggestion? Have a think about things
after you've had some sleep, then have a word with
Sister Harris. I'm sure the powers that be will find
some way of working round reduced shifts or something. They don't want to lose you, and you can't
afford to lose the job.'

Kara dredged up a smile, suddenly realising how
very tired she was. 'Yes, Sue. I promise I'll think
about it when I've had some sleep. And thank you

for being such a very special friend. You'll never know how much your support has meant…'

In spite of her exhaustion, it was some time before Kara fell asleep.

It wasn't the fault of the strangeness of the accommodation—she'd had an almost identical room as this in the nurses' block before she and Mac had moved in together.

It wasn't any immediate worries about Mac's condition either—before she'd tucked herself into the sleeping bag spread out on Sue's bed she'd phoned the unit and spoken to Alison about his condition.

No, the reason why she was wakeful when she should have been nearly instantly unconscious was because her brain insisted on replaying memories of happier times.

And every one of those happier times was filled with images of Mac.

Mac as he'd been the first time she'd ever met him…

A lean male hand had reached out to push the swing door at the same time as she had, and they'd collided in the doorway of the staff canteen.

He was nearly six feet tall to her five feet two and a bit, and the first time she'd looked up and up and up to meet his dark brown gaze she'd been captivated.

There'd been a glint of humour in his watchful eyes, like the glimmering of sunlight on the surface of a dark secret loch.

He had a lean, clever face, and the natural midnight darkness of his hair and lashes would have been the envy of many a cinema hero.

'Darroch MacGregor. Neurology,' he said with a

soft touch of his native Scots in his voice as he offered his hand.

'Kara Desmond. Obs and Gyn,' she replied, totally unconcerned that he held onto her hand long after it should have been politely released.

It was only the fact that they were blocking the entrance to staff waiting to go through for a meal that forced them to step aside. But he still hadn't relinquished his hold on her hand.

'You will share a meal with me,' he said, the words neither demand nor question but a simple statement of fact.

'Of course,' she replied, feeling as if she'd never need to eat again. There'd be no room with all the happy butterflies in her stomach.

They spoke non-stop, barely pausing to eat as they exchanged potted histories.

He told her about losing his small-town GP father during his first year at medical school after a brief, vicious battle with a fast-growing brain tumour. His very supportive mother survived until a year previously, too soon to see him become a consultant.

She told him about her minister father and his parish stalwart wife who had believed they were to remain childless until she'd arrived late in their lives. Unfortunately, that meant that now she, too, was without family…other than the instant family she'd acquired when she'd joined the staff at St Augustine's.

They both marvelled at the fact that they'd never bumped into each other before and made careful arrangements so that it would happen again soon…very soon.

She must have bored Sue silly over the next few

weeks with her sighing and grinning, but she was so deliriously happy and excited and every day just seemed to get better. Nothing remotely like this had ever happened to her before.

Anyway, as her feet didn't seem to touch the ground, there was nothing to bring her down to earth.

Kara was still smiling as she stretched, the happy memories from her dream following her into wakefulness.

'Mac,' she murmured sleepily, automatically reaching out one hand to his side of the bed. 'I was dreaming. Do you remember the time we—?' Her hand hit the cold wall at the side of Sue's single bed and suddenly reality crashed down on her with a vengeance.

'Oh, God, Mac,' she said in a strangled voice.

Suddenly the contrast between her memories of those earlier happy days was obscene when placed against his situation now.

She glanced at Sue's bedside clock and blinked in disbelief. Nearly twelve hours had gone by since she'd entered the room. How on earth could she have slept so long?

Trembling with a sudden sense of urgency she struggled out of the binding folds of the sleeping bag, completely unable to find the tab of the zip.

She went to reach for the pile of crumpled clothes she'd left on a nearby chair—the latest set of pale blue scrubs that Alison had found for her to wear however many days ago—and found they'd disappeared. In their place was a slightly bigger pile of her own clothes, the pair of jeans and the long-sleeved cotton shirt perfectly adequate for the temperature-controlled environment of Mac's ward.

'Dammit, Sue,' she muttered while she dragged each item on over clean underwear, hardly bothering to think about the fact that her friend must have gone to the flat to collect some of her things. There were more urgent matters on her mind. 'Oh, why didn't you wake me up when you brought these in?'

It didn't matter how fast she moved, something was telling her to move faster.

She didn't know what it was, but that something was screaming to her that it was important for her to get to Mac as soon as possible.

More than twelve hours had gone by since she'd sat beside him and held his hand. More than twelve hours since she'd spoken to him of her love and her belief that he'd come back to her.

What had happened in that time?

Had the sedatives worn off enough for Mac to return to consciousness?

She'd automatically reached for the borrowed sleeping bag to fold it away neatly but suddenly she couldn't bear another second's delay.

'Sorry, Sue,' she whispered as she whirled away from the rumpled bed and dismissed it from her mind. All she could think about was getting to Mac.

'Ah, Kara, I'm so glad you're here,' Professor Squires said gently as she finally skidded to a halt at the end of Mac's bed.

She was clearly out of breath and for just one moment she was convinced that her urge to hurry had brought her to the scene of good news. Why else would the professor be standing there with Alison and Gaynor, looking at Mac's case notes?

Then she saw his face and fear clenched a tight fist around her heart.

'What's happened?' she demanded, her pulse pounding so hard in her throat that it was nearly strangling her. 'Mac was stable when I phoned before I went to bed. I was asleep and no one phoned me. What's happened?'

'Sit down, my dear. Sit down,' he directed, apparently worried that she was going to collapse. He went to draw up a spare chair but Kara was already making her way past him to her usual post beside Mac, automatically reaching through the safety bars to take hold of his hand.

'Hello, Mac,' she murmured as she leaned forward to brush a soft kiss to his lips. She pressed her cheek to his and could tell that someone else had shaved him today. She'd missed out on that by sleeping so long. 'I'm back again, my love. Did you miss me?'

For several long seconds she stared at his face, shutting out everything around her as she memorised each feature all over again and searched for any changes.

Finally, she was ready to face the rest of them again, but nothing would make her relinquish her hold on his hand.

'What happened?' she asked quietly. 'Why didn't you take him off the sedatives? Did his brain start swelling again?'

'No, my dear,' the professor said quietly. 'We *did* take him off the sedatives.'

'You did?' she said and flicked a quick glance at Mac, lying so still and quiet. 'But…but why hasn't he woken up, then?'

The poor man looked genuinely unhappy but he didn't duck the issue.

'My dear, it looks as if Mac isn't going to be waking up. Ever since you left to get some sleep we've been hoping we would start to see some changes as the sedation was reduced. Unfortunately, he just seems to be slipping further and further away.'

'No!' Panic filled her. 'He can't be. He wouldn't.'

'My dear, you only have to look at the figures on his observations,' the eminent man tried to point out. 'Over the last few hours there should definitely have been some change in his response to testing. It's either that he can't or that he doesn't want to respond.'

'Doesn't *want* to respond?' Kara repeated, amazed at the thought. That didn't sound like Mac at all. Especially with her. They'd never been able to help their response to each other.

'I'm sorry, my dear, really I am, but—'

'Perhaps his responses weren't doing so well because I wasn't here with him,' she suggested on a sudden surge of hope. 'He was holding his own until I went away to sleep.'

'If only it were that easy,' he said with a tired smile. 'Unfortunately, it doesn't work that way.'

'Why not?' she demanded, her eyes flicking wildly from his sombre expression to the matching sympathetic looks she was receiving from Alison and Gaynor. 'The power of touch is always being underestimated and…and look!' She pointed at the monitor. 'His heart rate *has* changed since I returned.'

'A little,' he conceded, 'but on its own, it's just not enough. His pupils still don't respond to light, there are still no oculomotor responses to heat or cold, or any response to painful stimuli or noxious smells. My dear, there's never a *good* time, but it might be appropriate at this time for us to talk about whether you're willing to agree to his wish to be an organ donor.'

Kara was speechless with shock.

She knew Mac was registered on the computer system as a potential donor—she was, too—but never in her worst moments over the last four and a half days had she thought they'd come to this.

For several paralysed seconds she sat, staring at him, while the thoughts whirled around inside her head totally out of control.

If she were to permit the hospital to harvest Mac's organs after his death was pronounced, there could be seven people in the world whose lives would be improved, if not saved, by Mac. She knew this, and she knew, as many lay people possibly didn't, that time was of the essence if the organs were to be viable once they reached their new owner.

Still, everything inside her resisted the very idea.

'No! You can't have them,' she exclaimed suddenly, almost wildly. 'You can't have them because he still needs them himself. He's still alive.'

'My dear,' Professor Squires said patiently, apparently unruffled by her outburst, 'you must be realistic about it. You know the capacity of ventilators to perpetuate cardiopulmonary functions for long periods despite the failure of other body organs…even when there is a total absence of integrated brain function. Much as we sympathise, we can't just keep him on life support when there's no hope of recovery. Intensive care beds are expensive and in short supply'

'But…' Kara's heart was beating faster and faster as she saw the juggernaut heading straight for her, knowing that there was no way she could avoid a painful collision.

'Even though he could help many people if you would allow us to harvest his organs, we will obviously respect your decision, but it is my decision that we should complete the tests to have him declared legally brain dead.'

Kara's hand tightened convulsively around Mac's as the professor stated his position so baldly, but suddenly she felt icily calm.

'When will you do it?' she asked, her chin lifting a fraction as she tried to steel herself for the inevitable, whichever way the decision lay.

'Well, he's already off all anaesthetising or paralysing drugs and he's not hypothermic,' Professor Squires began patiently. 'So, if you'd like to wait outside, we'll do another check on his behavioural and reflex motor functions above the neck and then see if there's any spontaneous respiratory movement.'

Kara tightened her hands around Mac's and stiffened her shoulders.

'I want to stay with him,' she said quietly, her gaze unflinchingly on the professor.

'We usually prefer not to put relatives through the upset of watching,' he pointed out, 'but if you're certain?'

Kara swallowed hard and nodded. For Mac, she would cope with anything.

Silently she watched while Mac's eyes failed to respond in any way to either the glare of a bright light or the firm pressure of a swab on his cornea. Even when twenty millilitres of cold water was squirted deep in his ear there was no sign of an eye movement.

The acrid scent of old-fashioned smelling salts

nearly brought tears to her own eyes, but Mac was still unmoved, right up to the moment when the professor prepared to pass a suction catheter down his throat to check Mac's gag reflex.

Something clicked in Kara's memory, something that had happened yesterday, not long before she'd left Mac to go for her marathon sleep.

'Wait a moment,' she demanded suddenly, startling the eminent man as he concentrated on his sad task.

'Pardon?' He straightened up and gazed across at her on the other side of the bed.

'I'm sorry… Please…' She said hesitantly, and looked towards Alison. 'Have you got one of those mouth swabs we use for oral hygiene? The ones I was using yesterday.'

Alison was startled for a moment then reached for a pack of supplies on a nearby trolley.

'I'm sorry, Professor, I didn't mean to be rude, but when I saw what you were going to do it reminded me.' She was gabbling and she knew it, but if anything was to give Mac a chance… 'I've been helping to take care of Mac—washing him and shaving him and so on—and when I was using the swab yesterday I noticed something.'

She threw a distracted smile of thanks at Alison as she took the fresh swab from her.

'I was cleaning at the back of his teeth and took the swab just a little too far, but…' She had to stop talking for a moment because her voice was shaking. He was leaning over close to Mac, watching what she was doing in his mouth, and if she'd been wrong…

'One side, nothing happened, but on the other…' She was tempted to close her eyes and pray as she took the swab to the back of Mac's throat.

'Well, good gracious,' the professor murmured. 'Do you mind?' He took the swab from her and repeated what she'd done, his eyes narrowed in concentration.

'Well? That was a gag reflex, wasn't it?' Kara demanded, afraid to hope too much.

'It's very weak, but, yes, I have to admit it was.'

Kara drew in what felt like her first full breath in an hour and found that her hands were shaking.

'So what happens now?'

'Now we disconnect the ventilator,' he said quietly.

'Disconnect! But—'

'It's the standard test for apnoea,' he continued. 'We pre-oxygenate the patient by ventilating for ten minutes with one hundred per cent oxygen, then check the arterial pressure of carbon dioxide. If it's high enough to trigger the normal breathing response, we maintain the oxygen supply but disconnect him from the ventilator for ten minutes…and wait.'

Kara just felt numb as she watched the preparations going on around Mac, her only consolation the tight hold she had on their rings.

It didn't seem to matter how many hours she'd sat beside him, how many intimate things she'd had to do for him, she still hadn't become used to the idea that he wouldn't just open his eyes and speak.

Finally, everything was ready. Mac's carbon dioxide level was exactly right and the oxygen flow rate had been set at six litres per minute.

The ventilator was disconnected.

Suddenly, the absence of the regular sound that had permeated every second of Mac's existence since he'd been brought into this room left an immense gulf around him.

Where the hiss and hum of the machine had marked his continued survival, now there was a dreadful silence that hadn't been replaced by the sound of Mac's own breathing.

Kara tightened her hands around Mac's and brought it up to her mouth as she willed the man she loved to draw his first independent breath.

There was the right level of carbon dioxide in his system to trigger the response, but it needed healthy receptors in his brain to make the body's electrical system fire. If those receptors had been fatally injured in the crash...

'Come on, Mac, you can do it,' Kara murmured against his fingers, tears beginning to trickle down her cheeks as she saw the hand on the clock reach the thirty-second mark and sweep on towards a minute.

'Please, Mac. Please. You've got to try.'

With the ventilator disconnected he hardly looked ill. There was a definite layer of stubble growing over the side of his head where he'd been shaved, and the bruising from his broken nose was fading fast. His profile was almost perfect now that the old rugby injury had been corrected.

He looked a little paler and he'd definitely lost some weight since the accident but he'd soon gain that back when he —

'Oh, God, Mac. Don't leave me. Don't leave us. You can't. Not before you've seen our baby.'

The thought of giving birth and not having Mac beside her to tease her about whose eyes the baby had inherited or speculate on whether the child would be tall and athletic like him or petite and more artistic...

'Please Mac. Please…' She leaned forward and pressed her mouth to his, terrified that this would be the last time she ever felt his lips. 'I love you, Mac. Please…try…'

CHAPTER THREE

CAN'T... Can't do it... Not any more.

Tired... So terribly tired... So much easier not to try... Except...something...or someone...is calling... demanding...

Try... Please, try...

But it hurts... Oh, God, it hurts... And I'm just so...so tired... But something...someone...is calling. Someone is saying...try... Begging... Desperate...

'I told you so!' Kara sobbed through her tears as she watched Mac draw in yet another breath—his fourth, unaided, so far.

The professor shook his head, clearly moved in spite of the number of patients he must have seen in his career.

'I'm only sorry I couldn't do anything more directly for him,' he said softly, and touched one hand to her shaking shoulder. 'If it had been a surgical problem, a cancer, perhaps...'

'But it was your initial care that saved his life after the accident,' Kara pointed out, grateful that she could give praise where it was due.

'Well, I wish you all the best, my dear, because you're going to need it—both of you. This is only the first, very tiny step on a very long road, and none of us know how far along it Mac is going to be able to travel.'

* * *

Kara woke up with a start and stared up at the ceiling.

She was surprised to see that she was looking up at the ceiling in the flat—the one she shared with Mac—and suddenly realised that this was the first time she'd slept here in over a week.

It had undoubtedly been the worst week in her life, but for the first time since that phone call in the registrar's waiting room she had a really positive feeling about the future.

Today she had some tough decisions to make, but they couldn't be put off any longer.

Mac had been lucky enough to avoid fatal damage to the part of his brain that governed his automatic breathing response, as shown by his spontaneous efforts when the ventilator had been disconnected, but he was still in a very deep coma.

After the initial euphoria that Mac hadn't proved to be brain dead had faded a little, she'd requested an interview with Professor Squires.

In a harrowing hour, he'd laid out for her exactly how long the road stretched in front of Mac and how slowly it would have to be travelled if his brain wasn't to be damaged any further.

'People read the sensationalised newspaper accounts of coma patients recovering at the sound of their favourite pop star's voice or after being bombarded with flashing lights, and they believe that's all it takes to unlock the brain.' He sighed heavily. 'The fact that it's a billion times more complex than that isn't nearly as newsworthy.'

Kara's heart sank a little. She'd known from listening to Mac and Mike talking together that there were marvellous strides being made in applied clinical neurology. Unfortunately, the number of people specialising in that particular branch was minute, and there was no one close enough to be able to take charge of Mac's rehabilitation on a daily basis.

'The biggest problem you're going to face is that the one person who could have helped you to bring Mac out of this was Mac himself,' the professor added, mirroring her own thoughts.

'My special field has always been neurosurgery, particularly the removal of tumours from the brain and spinal cord. Now that I've lost Mac from my team, I'm going to have to replace him as quickly as I can for the sake of our patients.

'I don't have very high hopes that I'll be able to replace him with someone of his own calibre or expertise. There are too few of them and, offhand, I can't think of *any* other with a parallel ability in neurosurgery. Especially one who would be interested in moving to St Augustine's at such short notice.'

Kara nodded. She understood that the poor man had enough problems of his own, but that didn't mean that she was willing to let Mac suffer for lack of help.

The only person she knew who had the same interest in this field of neurology was Mike, and he'd promised to come down and visit the following weekend when he had some time off. Perhaps...

'Professor?'

The thoughts had been whirling round in her head as she'd said her goodbyes and she hadn't made her decision to ask until she was almost out of the door. Now she tightened her hold on their rings for courage.

'Yes, my dear?' He looked up at her from the open file on top of a mountainous stack.

'Professor, would you have any objection if Mac's friend, Mike Prowse, were to try to help Mac?'

His face flattened into that strangely watchful expression he sometimes wore when he was hiding his thoughts, and Kara was suddenly overwhelmed by a feeling of trepidation. Had she just done a very stupid thing? She couldn't afford to step on this man's toes. He was the only help Mac had at the moment.

'Do you mean that you would like to take Mac's care out of my hands?' he demanded quietly, a clear edge to his tone.

'No! Oh, God, no!' she exclaimed hastily, horrified that he should think such a thing. 'It's just that the two of them have the same interest in the way the brain works and I hoped…' Her voice broke and she had to wait a minute before she could continue. 'In the absence of a clone of Mac to help him on a daily basis, I was hoping that Mike could point me in the right direction so that I could do something to help him.'

She saw the professor blink in surprise.

'You?' he challenged with a growing frown. 'But you work in Obstetrics and Gynaecology.'

'I'm also the one with the most to lose if there's no one to give Mac the specific help he needs,' she pointed out quietly. 'I'll be going back to work because I have to earn my living, but that will only take forty hours a week. If I subtract another forty hours for sleeping, that still leaves eighty-eight hours to spend with Mac.'

'And you think you might as well be using that time to help him as merely keep him company?' he asked with a wry twist to his mouth.

He was silent for almost a full minute, his eyes very intent on her face while his brain worked, and it took all her determination not to squirm like a naughty pupil called for an interview with her headmaster.

Finally he broke the silence.

'Have you asked Mike Prowse whether he is willing to undertake this?'

'Certainly not,' she said quickly. 'They might be weird circumstances, with you as Mac's superior and his specialist, but it would still be against professional ethics for me to have done that.'

He nodded just once then reached for something on his desk and began to write.

'Well, then, perhaps you'd better approach him, and if he's willing to undertake the experiment, ask him to get in contact with me direct.' He held out a very plain white business card, his name and qualifications in small block letters across the front. 'I've put my private number on the back.'

Kara couldn't remember leaving the room, just the tremendous feeling of elation that filled her as she started walking away down the anonymous hospital corridor.

She managed to hold it in until she'd turned the first corner, then started walking faster and faster until soon she was running as fast as her feet would carry her.

Only consideration for staff and patients in this part of the hospital stopped her from whooping with joy, but she was doing it inside her head.

'Good morning, Kara. Welcome back,' said Sister Harris when Kara reported for her shift the next morning.

She was on early, starting at seven and finishing at

three, but she'd already been to visit Mac in his new room.

He was still wired up to an amazing battery of monitoring equipment, and was still on oxygen, but since those first painful breaths he hadn't needed to return to ventilator support.

Bearing in mind the slightly unusual course his treatment was going to take, the professor had suggested that the best option was to install Mac in one of the individual rooms just to one side of the department.

Later on this afternoon, Mike was going to be arriving for an interview with the professor and then his first visit to Mac since he'd come off the ventilator.

There was a real spring in her step as she made her way to the first of her charges this shift, the notes of a young Hispanic woman in labour with her first child tucked under one arm.

'Anna-Maria, my name is Kara,' she announced as she entered the noise-filled room, one of the newly refurbished suites that would be home to a patient right through her labour until delivery was completed.

Once she and her baby had been thoroughly checked and she was ready to join the rest of the new mothers, she would be moved to the more companionable atmosphere of a six-bed ward.

Not that she didn't have plenty of company with her now, Kara thought as she counted five adults in the room already. In fact there were so many of them, and all talking volubly at the top of their voices, that not only had the young woman not heard her introduction she probably hadn't seen her come into the room.

'Excuse me!' Kara called, deciding that was probably more polite than finding a referee's whistle to cut through the din.

Gradually, as one black-clad woman caught sight of her and nudged the person beside her, the noise abated until there was an almost unearthly silence.

'My name is Kara, and I'm your midwife, Anna-Maria,' she announced into the silence. 'I will need to examine you in a minute so I would be very glad if everyone would make their way to the waiting area.'

From silence to uproar in half a second, she thought in exasperation when the noise grew ten times worse than it had been before. This time there were arms waving in her direction as well, and all of it in a language she didn't pretend to understand.

With a fixed smile on her face she worked around the whole group like a champion sheepdog and herded them inexorably across the room and out of the door.

When it swung closed behind them she had to resist the urge to sink back against it with a sigh of relief. There was work to do, she thought as she pulled the file out from under her arm.

'Why did you sent my mama away?' demanded her patient with a sulky pout. 'She want to be with me so she can tell me how to have the baby. She know these things.'

'Is your mama a midwife?' Kara asked cheerfully, not wanting to tread on another professional's toes. She could hardly comment on the advisability of treating a member of your own family now that she was intending doing exactly that for Mac.

'No, but she have me,' the young woman said with childlike simplicity.

'And what about your husband? Does he know the baby is coming? Will he be with you when the baby's born?' Kara was adept at keeping up a conversation while she performed some of the more intimate tasks involved in the process of childbirth. She had yet to experience any of them for herself, but just the thought of submitting to a stranger's examination...

There was a telling silence from her voluble patient and she looked up to see a woebegone expression on her face. She seemed desperately young to be married and about to have a child; she was hardly more than a child herself.

'Mama send him away. Tell him to wait outside. She say babies are women's business. No place for man.'

The last sentence was forced out through gritted teeth as a contraction tightened its grip on her, and the young woman fought it every step of the way.

By the time it faded there was a sheen of sweat over every visible inch of skin and her glorious mane of dark hair was damp and tangled.

Kara set about making her charge more comfortable.

In the course of conversation she discovered that Anna-Maria was the very pampered only child of wealthy parents and had had the good fortune to fall in love with a young man her parents approved of.

Unfortunately, the fact that they'd signalled their approval by providing him with a job in the family import-export firm and a semi-separate apartment in the family home made for some tensions all round.

By the time the third contraction arrived, Kara had won enough of the young woman's trust to persuade her not to fight them.

She was a bright girl underneath all the spoiled-child pouting, and soon realised how much more manageable she was making the process for herself.

It didn't take long before she admitted that she wanted her husband with her when their child was born.

'But if you go out to tell him to come in then Mama will want to come too. And my grandmother and my godmother and my aunts. Do you know,' she added in amazement, 'my grandmother said he couldn't be near a new baby because he would injure the baby with the X-rays from his telephone?'

'X-rays? In a telephone?' Kara didn't dare laugh.

'It is what she believes,' Anna-Maria said simply. 'She will never touch one, not at her home in Spain, not here.'

'But your husband...?'

'He is modern. He has a mobile phone with him all the time so Papa can tell him what to do.'

Kara blinked as the picture of the young couple's daily problems became clearer. An idea began to grow.

'And he has his mobile phone with him now?' she asked.

'Yes. Always. Why?'

The reply had to wait while Kara coached her through the most powerful contraction yet.

'Do you think your husband—'

'Ramon,' she provided with a smile.

'Do you think Ramon wants to be with you when the baby is born?'

'Yes. But this isn't possible. Mama—'

'What Mama doesn't know...' Kara pointed out

with a grin and lifted the telephone. 'What's Ramon's number?'

In the end it was very simple.

Anna-Maria spoke to her husband, telling him to pretend the call was about work. Then she explained how he could leave the department by the lifts at one end and return by the stairs at the opposite end, out of sight of his gaggle of in-laws.

Kara watched a new bond being forged between the two of them over the next couple of hours, and when they proudly cradled their tiny daughter between them she felt tears threatening. It had been a rare thing to watch two young people mature so much in such a short time, and she hoped it augured well for the future of their little family.

She gave them as long as she could on their own but eventually it was time to face the thwarted crowd in the waiting room.

'*Señoras,*' she called to attract their attention, hoping her pronunciation was at least comprehensible. After all, her first Spanish lesson had lasted precisely five seconds, less than a minute ago. '*Esta una bambina.*'

If the smiles and wails and tears were anything to go by, she'd got the words right, she thought as she stood aside, giving up any hope of limiting the concerted charge to two visitors at a time.

'Phew, that was fun,' she joked when she returned to Sister Harris's office to report on the outcome.

'But tackled with your usual brand of tact and diplomacy,' Margaret Harris said, with her tongue firmly in her cheek. 'I don't know whether it was the godmother or the grandmother who wanted you delivered to the Spanish Inquisition.'

'Probably both, but as soon as I went in that room I realised that I was going to have to get rid of all of them until I found out what the patient herself really wanted.'

'I know.' Margaret held her hand up to stop Kara saying any more. 'I realised exactly what you were doing and why. That's why I told the older generation that you would only make them wait outside if it was important for the mother and the baby.'

'There'll probably be renewed demands that I face the Inquisition when they find out how we sneaked the husband in without them knowing,' Kara said with a chuckle. 'Poor kids. I don't think they have a single minute of privacy. How they're ever going to get that little baby into some sort of routine, with that crowd all wanting to pass her around, I don't know.'

'Well, that'll be their problem,' her superior pointed out. 'You've done your part in helping her to bring the little one out into the world. The rest is up to them.'

Kara had another delivery soon after that, a fifth baby for a very calm, very experienced older mum who hadn't arrived at the hospital until the contractions were nearly two minutes apart.

The fact that her husband had almost had to carry her in because she'd been determined to finish the housework first gave all three of them something to chuckle about over the next swift half-hour.

Kara's duties were almost entirely limited to monitoring progress and checking for the cord around the baby's neck. Mrs Ward was fit and strong and knew exactly what she was doing.

Her joyful reaction when she realised that, instead

of a fifth boy, she'd finally had the little girl she'd longed for made it even better.

The office was deserted when Kara returned there, and she took advantage of the fact to sit down quietly with a cup of tea.

She had no doubt that the rest of the staff were waiting for a chance to talk to her—so much had happened to her since they'd seen her last. But, just for a couple of minutes, she needed to sort through her own feelings about being back at work.

Kara hadn't realised how different it would feel to deliver a baby, knowing that there was a tiny being deep inside her who was gradually growing towards this day, too.

She placed a protective hand over her belly, smiling sadly. One of the most wonderful moments for a woman must be the moment when she told the man she loves that she's carrying his child. And so far she'd been denied that pleasure.

But one day…

She closed her eyes and concentrated on the image in her mind…the image of Mac cradling their child in his arms and smiling his thanks and love at her…

She had to have faith that one day it *would* happen, otherwise how would she go on?

This morning she'd seen a young couple still finding their feet as a family. She had no idea how Ramon and Anna-Maria would manage to carve some privacy for themselves, but she had a feeling that it would come.

As for Mrs Ward and her longed-for little girl, the sex of the baby almost seemed to have put the cherry on the top of that family's happiness.

For a moment it almost felt as though a fist tightened around her heart, and she realised that she felt almost jealous of the two families. For all their faults and problems, they *were* families, with other members to call on in times of need.

She and Mac only had each other, and with Mac so ill there was no one with whom she could share her worries for the future.

'Stop being a wimp,' she muttered as she pushed herself out of the chair. 'You're fit and healthy and carrying the child you'd hoped for—Mac's child. Even if, God forbid, Mac never comes out of the coma, you will still have a part of him that will live on.'

But it wouldn't come to that, she thought determinedly as she hurried towards the other end of the hospital. It was her lunch hour and she'd grabbed some sandwiches and a bottle of fresh juice to eat on the run so that she could spend more time with Mac.

'Hello, my love,' she said as she pulled a seat up beside his bed, less self-conscious about speaking aloud to him now he'd been moved into this side room.

She reached for his hand and wrapped her own around it as she leaned forward to kiss him.

Each time she did it she hoped it would be the time his lips responded to hers, but he stayed still and quiet. At least he was warm to the touch, as if he were merely sleeping heavily.

'Mike's coming to see you on Friday,' she told him and began fishing in her uniform pocket when she remembered the list she'd stuffed in there first thing this morning. 'He's given me a whole lot of things to do to you to help him decide what the next step is.'

She bent her head to decipher her scribbles then straightened again.

'First, your nails,' she announced. 'I've got to do each hand separately and each foot, too. I've got to press on a nail so that the bed goes white, then see how long it takes the capillaries to refill.'

She worked her way around him, talking all the while about what she was doing and her findings.

'Next, I've got to see if I can give you goose-bumps, although in the warmth of this room that might be difficult.'

She wetted two tissues with cold water and smeared them over the smooth skin of his upper arms. It was a little difficult to make sure that she was blowing equal streams of cold air over the wet patches, but the results were very clear.

'I'm getting the same results with every test, Mac,' she said as she repeated the cold-water test on his legs. 'With the water I'm seeing the goose-bumps appearing very much more on one side than the other, and with your nails the capillary refill was very much faster on one side of your body.'

She settled herself back beside him and threaded her fingers between his, carefully keeping an eye on the time.

'I've been reading up a bit in some of your books,' she told him. 'It seems as if that lopsided gag reflex I discovered was only the first indication of what's going on inside your brain. Now I've started finding these others, it will help Mike to decide the best way to persuade your brain to repair itself.'

She raised his hand to her lips and pressed a kiss to each knuckle, drawing in a shuddering sigh when she realised that, in spite of all the surrounding medicinal odours, she could still detect the scent of his skin.

'In the meantime, just so you don't think I've deserted you when you don't hear me talking to you, he's suggested that I play you that CD of Mozart I gave you for Christmas.'

The disc was supposed to be relaxing, which was why she'd bought it for him. It wasn't her fault that the first time he'd listened to it they'd ended up making passionate love on the settée, then falling off onto the floor and continuing there, too.

It had become a joke between them to mention to their colleagues that they were going home to put that 'relaxing' CD on—knowing full well what would happen as soon as they heard the familiar strains.

In their flat, the music had served as partial camouflage for their activities, to give them some privacy from their neighbours. In Mac's hospital room it would only be played very softly as the last thing his delicately balanced system needed was to be overloaded by volume.

'Time to go now,' she said softly when the clock hands clicked round, still hating to leave him when he was so helpless. 'I promise I'll be back as soon as my shift ends.'

She bent forward to kiss him, running her fingers carefully over the silky prickles of his swiftly regrowing hair. With the stitches out now, the scar had flattened a little more, and once his thick, dark thatch was back to its normal length it would probably completely hide the site of the injury.

She was on her way out of the department when there was a bit of a stir by one of the other beds.

Kara vaguely remembered that the man had been

brought in at roughly the same time as Mac, but she'd been too busy worrying about *him* to take much notice of the other patients.

'I'm going, now, Joanne,' she said, letting the person on duty on Mac's team know she was leaving his room.

There was a brief clatter on the other side of the room and they both looked across.

'Problem?' Kara asked when the curtains were drawn closed around that bay.

'He didn't make it,' Joanne said softly, careful that her voice didn't carry. 'Too many injuries—head, neck, and chest—plus he was overweight, a drinker and a smoker.'

'Poor man,' Kara murmured. She was far too close to a similar tragedy of her own not to sympathise. 'How did it happen?'

Joanne glanced at her, as though wondering whether she should say anything. 'Road accident. Apparently, he was in too much of a hurry and tried to jump the lights.'

'Oh, God.' Just like Mac's accident. 'Was anyone else hurt?'

Joanne hesitated again, but this time she didn't seem to be able to meet Kara's eyes.

It took a couple of seconds, but suddenly the penny dropped.

'Oh, God, it was him, wasn't it?' Kara whispered behind her hand. 'He was the one who hit Mac.' She wasn't a vengeful person and was appalled by the sudden feeling that, with the man's death, justice had been done. It would be no consolation if Mac didn't recover.

Before Joanne could answer either way, the curtain

on the other side of the room swished back and a woman several years younger than Kara's twenty-seven was ushered out.

Even at this distance Kara could see that she was devastated, her eyes bruised hollows in her deathly pale face.

'Is that his wife?' she whispered, all too easily able to imagine how the woman was feeling.

On the odd occasion that she'd thought about the man who had done this to Mac, she'd thought she would hate him and anything connected with him.

Seeing the effect his death was having on his poor, innocent wife showed her the other side of the coin.

Before she'd consciously thought about it her feet were taking her across the room towards the devastated woman.

'Are you here by yourself?' she asked gently, limiting her impulse to cupping the woman's shaking arm.

'Dad dropped me off on his way to work. There's…there's only me and him now,' she whispered.

'Come through to the office and phone him. You shouldn't be alone,' Kara suggested.

The father must have been expecting the worst because he arrived swiftly to wrap his grieving daughter in his arms.

As he led the young woman away from the department, Kara found half of her emotions empathising with her grief while the other part raged inside her head that at least *that* young woman still had a father to support her. If the worst happened to Mac…

She refused to think about it, concentrating on the fact that Mike would be there soon.

There was also her job to bolster her spirits. She'd been worried about her concentration, concerned that she might be too preoccupied with worrying about Mac to do her job properly.

In practice, it seemed to be working the other way. When she was working with one of her charges, helping them to bring a new life into the world, she found it easy to concentrate. She'd always been awed at being part of the miracle of birth, and now that miracle seemed in some way to soothe her soul.

Anyway, she preferred to be busy, which was why she was so grateful that the team looking after Mac had allowed her to help. It didn't matter that the tasks she was taking on could mean that she was busy almost continuously for sixteen hours a day. It was better than sitting alone in the flat with her memories and her fears.

Not that she would be able to keep the flat for very long, she thought as she calculated her finances. It would probably be cheaper and easier if she moved back into the hospital's staff accommodation. It would only take her minutes to get to work or to be by Mac's side, and until he was ready to leave the hospital for good she didn't like living so far away and all by herself.

A double bed was far too big for one when you'd grown used to sharing, she thought sadly. She allowed just a brief glimpse of happy memories to lift her heart and bolster her determination that those good times *were* going to return.

CHAPTER FOUR

'MIKE'S here,' Sue said with more than friendly interest in her voice.

Kara threw her friend a swift glance. She'd suspected that it hadn't been just altruism that had Sue keeping her company this evening, and the becoming colour blooming in her cheeks was clear evidence of that.

'Hi, Sue. Hi, Kara. How's he been?'

'Never mind that for a minute. How did your talk go with the professor?' Kara demanded. She'd been on pins all day about the meeting between Mac's friend and the head of the department.

If Mike thought she could hold her tongue through a round of social niceties…

'It went well, Kara,' Mike said quietly, placing one of his hands over hers where they held Mac's. 'A lot of the work that Mac and I have been doing over the last few years is a long way outside normal hospital clinical practice, and the professor had to be certain that he wouldn't be doing Mac a disservice by allowing my input.'

'But it's neurology,' Kara began.

'It's functional clinical neurology,' Mike corrected patiently. 'It's a very precise new field, studying a very imprecise organism—a human being. A lot of the work being done is still very experimental, but some of the results have been nothing short of spectacular.'

'And it's the results we want for Mac,' Kara said, as she fished in her pocket for the piece of paper detailing the results of the tests she'd done on Mac. 'Here are the observations you wanted me to do, with the capillary refill on his nails and the goose-bumps with the cold water.'

Kara had told Sue what Mike had asked her to do so she didn't need to explain now.

'Good. That's exactly what I expected you to find,' Mike said, as he looked at the little stick figure diagrams Kara had drawn and the accompanying numbers.

'So what does it mean?' Kara demanded. 'Why would his reactions be so much more marked on one side of his body than the other, and why should the stronger response be on opposite sides for each set of tests?'

'Because the muscular control of each side of the body is controlled by the opposite side of the brain, while the circulation is controlled by the same side,' Mike said simply.

'So, in a stroke affecting the left side of a person's body, the damage is actually on the right side of the brain, but it causes problems with the blood control systems on the right side of the body?'

'Exactly. That's why, with this injury to the right side of Mac's brain, you're finding the goose-bumps reflex weakened on his left side while his capillary refill is slower on the right. You've probably also noticed that his right side is slightly bluer in appearance.'

'So, what can we do to even them up? Should he be having extra physiotherapy on that side to speed it up?'

'No. That's actually the last thing he needs.' Mike paused for a moment, his forehead creased in thought. 'The best way I can think to describe it is for you to imagine that Mac's brain is a coach harnessed to a pair of horses, one on the right and one on the left.'

He grabbed a piece of paper and drew a quick sketch.

'The situation at the moment is that one horse is galloping as fast as he can to try to pull the coach because the other one can't pull his weight. The galloping horse can only keep it up for so long before he'll collapse, exhausted.'

'So we have to slow the galloping horse down?' she suggested.

'Unfortunately, if *he* stops working, the carriage won't be going anywhere.'

'So we have to force the other horse to do his own share of the work?'

'No, because that poor horse isn't fit to take the load, so once again you'd end up with the carriage going nowhere at all.'

'So what *do* we do?' Kara demanded, frustrated when it seemed as if there was no way out.

'Imagine that the injured horse is like any other athlete. If you want him to race, you have to get him well and in training so that the first time you ask him to work he's actually fit enough to do the job, without breaking down. Then, when the galloping horse realises that his partner is fit and able to share the load, he will gradually slow down of his own accord until they're dividing the job between them again.'

'How do we do it? We can hardly take one half of his brain out and take it to a gym,' she exclaimed.

'Actually, you've already started the work,' Mike

pointed out, calming her with little more than the tone of his voice. 'You've been talking to him and touching him and playing soft music. Everything soft and gentle.'

'And nothing's been happening,' Kara said. 'I know his gag reflex is still working more strongly on one side than the other from when I do his oral hygiene, but that's all.'

'That's good,' Mike insisted. 'It would be very easy to trigger his brain into providing you with concrete proof that other reflexes can be made to perform, but it would massively overload the system and burn it out completely. For ever.'

Kara was shaken by the finality of the words and silently vowed to be more patient.

'Is there anything else she can do?' Sue asked quietly. 'I can understand why she's feeling frustrated.'

'Then she'll have to get used to the feeling,' Mike said plainly. 'There's no guarantee that Mac's going to come out of this, no matter how slowly and carefully we take it, but I can virtually guarantee that if we try to hurry it we'll lose him.'

Kara swallowed down a feeling of nausea that had nothing to do with her pregnancy, then straightened her shoulders. Now that she knew what the danger was, she'd just have to accept the slow pace as a necessity.

'OK, Mike. Slowly and cautiously it is,' she agreed quietly. 'Do I just continue with the music and talking and holding his hand or is there anything else you want me to do?'

'Have you been with Mac when the physiotherapist's been here?' he asked. His hands were busy checking the relative range of movement of Mac's feet and the comparative muscle tone.

'A couple of times. She's talked me through what she's trying to do so I can do it for him. Why?'

'Tell me what she's shown you,' he directed, and stood aside.

'Well, she said that one of the problems with people in long-term comas is that they suffer from disuse atrophy. She was putting each of his limbs through a series of movements and stretches so he won't lose his mobility.'

'Gentle stretches?' he clarified. 'And always in the same order?'

'Yes. Gentle stretches, but she didn't say anything about the order in which they should be done.'

'Right, then. I've just been doing a few comparative tests on Mac to work out the best way to begin. Obviously, what we'll do for him is absolutely individual to his injuries and would be unlikely to be exactly right for any other coma patient.'

He grasped Mac's left foot and stroked it, before stretching his toes gently upwards towards his knee.

'This is how I want you to start,' he said. 'This will fire his stretch receptors in his muscles to fire into his brain. Then follow through the gentle exercises the physiotherapist showed you, but finish the session with another gentle stretch of that left foot. Each time, start with that foot and finish with the same foot.'

'And should I be doing any testing to see if it's making any difference?'

'Do as little direct testing as possible because each time you're taking the brain very close to overload. Give it time to heal and grow new pathways to replace those lost in the accident.'

'But surely we need to know if we're on the right path? How will we know if we don't check?'

'When you plant seeds, do you keep digging them up every day to see if they've started growing?' he retorted sharply. 'Kara, you're going to have to trust me on this. There is nothing I wouldn't do to help Mac recover, believe me. With neurology, one of the most difficult parts of the Hippocratic oath to keep is that we shall do no harm to our patients. How can you not destroy brain cells when you're trying to remove an invasive cancer?

'But in Mac's case, because of the injury, we've got to be extra careful not to gork any more cells. If we take it gently enough we'll be helping him to form new connections to centres that can take over the jobs of the cells that have died.'

'So I start off by stretching his left foot up slowly like this,' Kara said, wrapping both hands around Mac's naked foot and stretching his toes upwards. 'Then I can continue working on the rest of the ligaments and muscle groups for each of his limbs, finishing up with exactly the same slow stretch.'

'You've got it. And if you pass it on to the physiotherapist and each of the nurses who have to do any work with him—for example when he's washed—tell them to follow the same routine. Start and finish with that foot.'

'And the music and the talking?'

'Continue with that, but try not to let it become predictable. You need to have something new to gently stimulate the right side of his brain because that's where new experiences are processed—new sounds, new smells, new feelings and tastes. Not too many at once but, for example, change your perfume,

stroke him with silk or wool as well as your hand or
his towel, touch him with a cold flannel sometimes in
between the warm ones. Just on a small area at first,
on his leg or arm—not his hand or foot because there
are too many receptors concentrated there and you'll
be blasting his brain with a foghorn when a whisper
will do.'

Kara had needed to feel she was doing something
to help Mac, and all of a sudden it seemed as if there
was so much to do that there couldn't possibly be
enough hours in the day to accomplish it all.

Mike promised to return in a few days to check on
her progress and then Sue volunteered to keep him
company while he grabbed a quick meal.

Kara threw Sue a quick thumbs-up sign as the two
of them left the side room, and saw her friend's
cheeks grow pinker.

'Well, good luck to her,' she murmured as she
reached for her handbag and took out the small note-
pad she'd taken to keeping in there. There were a few
notes she wanted to make to herself before she forgot
all the ideas that had swarmed through her brain while
Mike had been talking.

There were several more CDs she could bring in
to give Mac some variety in his listening, one or-
chestral selection and one of Spanish guitar music for
a start.

There was also that little set of perfume miniatures
that Sue had given her for Christmas last year. She'd
been carefully saving them for special occasions, but
they would certainly be put to good use if they helped
to stimulate Mac's brain to recover.

'What about tastes?' she murmured, wondering exactly how she could vary them when Mac wasn't able to eat normally.

She remembered what Mike had said about the number of receptors on Mac's hands and feet and then remembered that the tongue was even more abundantly supplied with nerves.

'So it doesn't have to be very much,' she reasoned. 'Just the tiniest taste on his tongue should be enough—like a drop of orange juice, or lemon, or I could wipe a slice of a strawberry over his tongue.'

Her thoughts took off with ideas for tastes of pepper and curry and chocolate.

'We're going to get there, my love,' she whispered as she kissed him goodbye when it was finally time for her to go back to the flat. 'It might take a long time, but we'll be together again.'

'Kara, do you need me to take over for you?' Sue offered through the closed door.

She'd just followed Kara into the staff toilets in time to hear her being violently sick.

It was several minutes before Kara could catch her breath enough to answer her.

'Don't be silly. You've only just finished your shift,' she said on a groan as her stomach rebelled again.

'Well, can I get you anything?' Sue offered. 'What about a decaffeinated coffee?'

Just the thought of the smell was enough for Kara.

'Water,' she gasped. 'Plain water and a plain biscuit.'

'Hey, does that plain biscuit trick really work?' Sue asked.

'Don't know, but at least it gives you something to

bring up,' Kara said grimly, barely daring to move in case everything started again.

She'd been worried that she might be one of those women who put on a lot of extra weight during a pregnancy. At just over five feet two inches it was something she'd always had to be careful about.

She needn't have worried. What with spending every spare off-duty minute with Mac and being sick for weeks on end, she'd actually lost weight in the last three months. If she didn't stop being sick soon, she'd be fading away to a shadow.

'I'll be all right,' she said with her fingers crossed, and flushed. 'It's my own fault. I was in such a hurry to see Mac this morning that I didn't stop to have anything to eat first.'

She rinsed her face and hands and accepted the plastic cup of water Sue was holding out to her.

'So what was the big hurry?' Sue folded her arms and leant back against the edge of the sink. 'You're already spending endless hours beside him as it is.'

'Didn't Mike tell you?' Kara exclaimed, amazed in view of the fact that Mike and Sue seemed to be spending a lot of time together these days.

'I haven't seen him since I went on duty,' Sue said primly.

'Well, what a surprise! I thought the two of you had been joined at the hip since Mike took the job on the professor's team,' Kara teased.

It had been a totally unexpected development, but Mike seemed to have impressed Professor Squires so much that he'd actually approached Mike with the offer of a job on his team at St Augustine's.

Kara hadn't known who'd been more delighted, Sue because the object of her steadily growing affections was going to be so much closer, or Kara herself because Mike would be able to see Mac on a daily basis.

She'd been diligently following Mike's directions while she'd been helping to take care of Mac, but she'd always felt that he would progress far faster if Mike was there on the spot.

And it seemed as if she'd been right.

'Last night, just before I was going to leave him to go to bed, I was playing that CD with the guitar music. There's one track that's so soft and gentle it was almost sending me to sleep. I turned to say something to Mac and I suddenly noticed that his eyes were moving, just as if he was dreaming.'

'Oh, Kara! I'm so pleased for you,' Sue exclaimed, after all this time knowing exactly what significance that had for Kara. 'What did Mike say?'

'He did some very careful testing and he found that, apart from his gag reflex getting stronger and a weak jaw reflex returning, Mac now reacts slightly to the pain of smelling salts and has a slight corneal reflex.'

'Oh, Kara!' Sue wrapped her in an exuberant hug. 'I definitely think we need to celebrate with a dry biscuit or two.'

'Trust you to keep my feet on the ground,' Kara grumbled. 'I was so excited this morning that I wasn't certain whether I'd dreamed it last night.'

Sue left a little while later and, after nibbling slowly at several plain biscuits, Kara was ready for what promised to be a very busy day.

She had three ladies to keep an eye on at the moment, all of them approaching the upper end of their child-bearing years.

One lady was in labour with her twelfth child, while each of the other two was having their first.

'Twelve!' she'd exclaimed when she'd first read the file, certain that there must have been a clerical error.

'That's right, and every one of them planned,' said her husband proudly. 'This one will be a girl to complete the set.'

Kara caught the twinkle in Mrs Marshall's eye and gave her an answering smile. She was having enough difficulty contemplating the arrival of one child. What must it be like, knowing you were going to take the new baby home to a tribe of waiting brothers and sisters? She didn't know whether to envy her or not.

The other two ladies, although they were in the same situation, couldn't have approached it with more different attitudes.

'I didn't want this baby from the first,' Mrs Taylor-Deane said angrily when the pethidine didn't work instantly. 'I was due to go on holiday—a cruise in the Seychelles with friends. Now look at me! I'll never get my figure back after this, and we'll have to employ a nanny or we'll never get away for a holiday again!'

Mrs Fry barely needed any pain relief, she was just so ecstatic that her longed-for child was finally about to be born.

'Twenty-seven years I've waited,' she confided to Kara between contractions. 'We've never taken any precautions against having children but it just never happened. Then when my monthlies stopped completely I just cried for weeks, thinking it was never going to happen. I was so certain I was going through the change, you see.'

She gave an almost girlish giggle. 'I couldn't believe it when the doctor tested me and told me I was pregnant. Poor man, I don't think one of his patients has ever lifted him up and swung him round before!'

Kara chuckled. 'Well, you have to do something, don't you?' she agreed. 'Why not terrorise a GP or two?'

'He insisted on doing all the tests to make sure the baby didn't have spina bifida and so on, but I told him it wouldn't make a blind bit of difference if it did,' Mrs Fry said firmly. 'Whatever the baby looks like won't matter. It's my baby and I've got twenty-seven years' worth of love waiting for it.'

Kara knew what she meant. When she'd first met Mac and fallen in love with him it had felt the same—as if she had a lifetime's worth of love waiting just for him.

All three ladies were progressing slowly but surely towards the second stage of labour, and Kara was beginning to worry that all three were going to need her undivided attention at once when Mrs Marshall pressed her buzzer.

'Could you check me, please?' she asked quietly. 'I really feel as if I want to start pushing now.'

Kara should have known that a veteran of eleven previous deliveries would know what she was doing. It was only a matter of seconds before she was able to give her the all-clear.

'I'm sure this was much easier when I was younger,' she puffed between pushes.

'It certainly doesn't help when you insist on growing such big babies,' Kara pointed out. 'Most people produce them at about the three- to three-and-a-half-kilo size. You manage anything from four to five and a half, and you're such a little thing.'

'It helps if they get a good start,' Mr Marshall added, his wife's hand held firmly in his. 'Then about nine months of good feeding to set them up for the rest of their lives.'

In less than an hour Mr Marshall was bearing his little daughter off for her first bath while Kara waited for the delivery of the placenta.

'So he was right about the sex of the baby,' she commented to her patient.

'He always is,' she said with a smile. 'And he only missed being here for the birth with one of them.'

'You're a very lucky woman,' Kara said sincerely, unable to help wondering if Mac would even have emerged from his coma by the time their child was born.

'It helps if you choose the right man first time,' Mrs Marshall said serenely. 'It was seven years between the day I met my husband and when I married him, but I knew he was worth waiting for. I haven't regretted it a single day.'

Once Mrs Marshall was ready, Kara directed her removal to the quiet ward right at the end of the unit.

'You'll be on your own for a while until my other two ladies deliver, but I think you'll be good for them,' she said quietly. 'They're both first-time mums.'

'I should be able to show them the ropes, after all the practice I've had,' Mrs Marshall said sleepily. 'I just hope it doesn't scare them to death when my mob arrives at visiting time. They're quite likely to adopt any stray babies on sight so there are enough to go round for cuddles.'

Kara laughed at the idea.

'I'd like to see that. I'll make a point of sticking my head round the door if I'm still on duty.'

She left the woman to have a well-deserved sleep to get her strength up. If she didn't miss her guess, once Mrs. Marshall had recovered from the birth that enormous baby was going to wake up demanding food every couple of hours. She was nearly as big as a three-month-old child already.

She sighed as she made her way back towards Mrs Taylor-Deane's room, wondering if *her* poor child would ever get fed—then rebuked herself for the uncharitable thought.

Once the baby arrived and the bond was formed, the woman would probably end up being every bit as good a mother as the others.

Not that you could tell it now, Kara thought darkly as she had to endure yet another round of complaints.

'I told the doctor I didn't want it,' the labouring woman repeated for the umpteenth time. 'I told him I wanted an abortion, but he said there was no valid reason for killing a child. No valid reason? The fact that it's completely ruining my life isn't a valid reason?'

Kara had reached her limit.

'Well, then, why don't you put it up for adoption as soon as it's born?' she suggested sharply. 'There are thousands of couples who can't have a child who would welcome yours with open arms.'

She had a feeling that only the advent of a particularly strong contraction saved her from another mouthful of invective. As it was, Mrs Taylor-Deane was definitely out of breath by the time she replied.

'The very idea!' she exclaimed. 'With everyone on

the committee knowing I'm pregnant, how could I go home and tell them I'd put the baby up for adoption? Half of them went ridiculously gooey-eyed when I had to tell them I wasn't just putting on obscene amounts of fat.'

Kara was glad that the woman's husband arrived just then, full of the details of a successful business meeting. By the time she'd directed him into a gown and he was back at his wife's side, her labour had suddenly started to speed up.

'God, I hate this,' she panted, just as the head was crowning. 'I'm all sweaty and out of breath and I must look like a beached whale.'

'Darling, you've never looked more magnificent,' Mr Taylor-Deane said suddenly, completely startling his wife—as well as Kara. 'I always knew you were a strong woman—you've had to be to work with me to build the business up from nothing. But this… To rise to such a challenge…' He shook his head, apparently lost for words.

'Rise to a challenge?' the woman muttered with a new gleam in her eyes as she drew in another breath to push. 'I'll show you rise to a challenge.'

In a matter of minutes a little boy weighing just over three kilos was yelling furiously at his rude entrance into the world.

As Kara settled her into the ward with Mrs Marshall she didn't doubt that there would be intermittent fireworks from the outspoken woman, but she had a feeling that Mrs Marshall would take it all in her stride.

That just left Mrs Fry, still puffing and panting her way through interminable contractions with the Entonox mask clutched tightly in her hand.

'How are you doing, Mrs Fry?' Kara asked as she checked the poor woman's blood pressure again.

'You tell me,' she gasped. 'I know I've wanted this for so many years, but I've suddenly realised why it's called labour.'

'At least there's an end to it eventually. And all the other mums say that they don't remember the pain when they've got their baby in their arms.'

'I'll hold you to that,' she retorted with a mock glare. 'I take it you haven't gone through this your-self?'

'Not yet,' Kara admitted, her hand straying to the tell-tale curve that had started to appear just below her waist.

'You're pregnant!' Mrs. Fry's eyes lit up with plea-sure. 'When's your baby due?' She gasped and turned to her husband. 'You have no idea how good it feels to ask another woman that without feeling the least bit jealous.'

Kara joined in their laughter.

'It's not due till some time early in the New Year, and I can honestly say I'm not in the least bit jealous of what you're going through now.'

She was beginning to be a little concerned about Mrs Fry's slow progress. At her age it would be very easy for her to become too exhausted to expel the baby. If the child became wedged in the birth canal there would be a danger that the oxygen supply could be compromised.

The last thing she needed after waiting so many years to have a child was for the infant to become brain-damaged during birth.

'Sister Harris. Can I have a word?' Kara was lucky

to catch the senior sister on her way to her office as she came out of Mrs Fry's room.

While Kara outlined her concerns Margaret Harris automatically reached over to switch the kettle on, the action as instinctive as the way she always set out two cups and invited her juniors to share a few minutes' break.

'How's the baby standing up to labour?' she probed, silently holding up milk with a questioning lift of an eyebrow.

'His pulse is dipping with each contraction, but nothing worrying so far. It's just…she's forty-eight years old and she's never had a baby before. She's so desperate for this one that if anything happened to it…' She grimaced, knowing she didn't need to say any more for Margaret Harris to understand.

'So are you suggesting we put a drip up to give her a bit of help, or are you thinking she might need surgical intervention?'

'I don't think it will come to surgery unless something goes radically wrong,' Kara said quickly. 'Would it be an idea, in view of her age, if we grabbed whoever's on duty and got them to have a quick look at her under the guise of a social call?'

'I think it would be a wise precaution, and not just because I've got a soft spot for her too.' She handed Kara the cup of tea she preferred now that she was pregnant and settled herself into her chair with a sigh of relief. 'Now, then, tell me about Mac's progress,' she invited.

Kara knew that the rest of the staff were concerned about the ongoing situation, but it had been going on for months now and most of them had stopped asking.

It was obvious from her detailed questions and her

response to the recent news that her superior really cared.

'So you're really beginning to see evidence that the coma is starting to lighten?'

'You'd have to have seen him before to recognise the differences now, but, yes, it seems as if the softly softly approach is finally working.'

'Keep it up, my dear,' she encouraged quietly. 'I've got a strong feeling you're going to win in the end.'

'Well, I hope poor Mrs Fry is,' Kara said, wary of allowing her emotions too much free rein in case she couldn't regain control. Sometimes it seemed as if it had been years since she'd been able to allow herself to relax.

At least she could always lose herself in her work, she thought a little later as she set up a drip to deliver a uterine stimulant to speed Mrs Fry's labour along.

Because she'd had a tendency towards high blood pressure during her pregnancy, she was being given oxytocin rather than ergometrine, but in either case Kara would monitor the dosage carefully to prevent excessively violent contractions.

It didn't take long for the drug to start working, and where progress had previously been measured in millimetres, now it was in centimetres. At last the cervix was fully dilated and Mrs Fry could begin to push her baby out into the world.

It was another hour before Kara was able to lay a little daughter in the exhausted woman's arms.

'Hello, little one,' she heard the new mother whisper, with tears streaming down her cheeks. 'There's only one name for you, and that's Miriam because it means wished-for child.'

CHAPTER FIVE

THE voice was back again. Her voice.

So many times there was noise drifting in and out but the darkness was always there and he could always retreat into the darkness...

Except when she was there.

He didn't know whether to resent her or not, but her voice seemed to be the only sound that could lift the blackness—that and her touch...

Soft. Gentle. Insistent.

It would be so much easier just to drift...but she wouldn't let him.

For some reason she seemed determined to drag him out of the peaceful darkness towards the pain of the light.

'Come on, Mac. Try,' Kara panted as she lifted one long leg straight up in the air to stretch his hamstrings.

She couldn't help noticing that, after all these months of immobility, he'd lost much of the muscle bulk he'd developed during his years of playing rugby.

She ran both hands over the rough curling hairs on his calf and up onto his thigh, silently thinking that, even so, he still had legs to be proud of. Long and lean and straight, giving an overall impression of power. It wouldn't take long, once he came out of the coma, for him to re-train the muscles again.

She couldn't help remembering the first time she'd seen Mac without his clothes.

'You'd been out running, remember?' she said softly as she transferred her attention to his other leg and began to work on those muscles and ligaments. 'It had rained heavily while you were out, and you looked like a drowned rat when you nearly knocked me over.'

She smiled at the memory.

She'd sidestepped in a hurry and had narrowly avoided stepping straight off the pavement into an enormous puddle when he'd grabbed her elbow to steady her. Unfortunately she hadn't been able to avoid the taxi going past as it had showered her with gallons of icy water.

She hadn't realised that he'd lived just a few doors away until he'd invited her in to get dry.

'I should have known from the wicked twinkle in your eyes that it was just an excuse to get my clothes off,' she teased softly. 'How you managed to keep a straight face when you told me the shower would be warmer if we shared it, I'll never know.'

What she *had* known had been that she hadn't wanted to resist him, and she'd been only too willing to follow his lead when he'd offered to share his soap with her and when he'd wrapped his arms around her and carried her, still dripping wet, to his bed.

Kara was trembling when she finished her mobilisation routine with that final important stretch of Mac's left foot.

It wasn't so much the physical effort involved, although it was quite a strain, wielding his long arms and legs when he wasn't able to help her. The biggest problem these days were the suppressed emotions that fought for release every time she relived a fresh batch of memories for Mac.

It would be easy to blame Mike.

He'd pointed out that certain centres in a man's brain are more primitive and could therefore be used as a window into the system to stimulate other areas.

At first she hadn't believed that there was a centre that could almost be termed the 'blue joke' region in a man's brain, but he'd assured her it was true.

She'd found it almost impossible at first—it would have been totally impossible if he had still been in a bed surrounded by others—but at Mike's urging she had gradually been able to make herself 'talk basic' with him.

The trouble was, so far she had no evidence to show that it was having any effect on Mac, but far too much evidence that it was having an effect on herself.

The fact that she was pregnant only seemed to make it worse.

At her last antenatal check-up she'd been chatting to a couple of the other mums who'd been teasing each other about the effect of rampant hormones on their sex lives. Kara hadn't fully understood what they'd been talking about until Mike had persuaded her to undertake this next stage in Mac's neurological treatment.

At the time Kara had smiled at the expression 'all hot and bothered' when it had been bandied about by heavily pregnant women, but that's certainly how she was feeling after each session with Mac.

She stood up and stretched her arms to relieve the tension, feeling a dull ache in the small of her back that warned her she'd forgotten about the presence of another little person while she'd been working on Mac.

It was time she took a walk around to straighten out the kinks. Perhaps she could have a chat with the people in the department whom she'd grown to count as her friends over the passing months. Or perhaps one of the other family members needed a listening ear while they voiced their all-too-similar fears for the future.

'I'm just going out for a minute, Mac,' she told him, following Mike's advice to behave as if Mac could hear and understand her every word. She knew that many studies of coma and near-death patients had confirmed that the senses of hearing and touch were usually the last to go and the first to return. 'I'll be back as soon as I've stretched my legs.'

As usual she bent forward to kiss him, and as usual paused briefly in the hope that this time he would respond.

She sighed and straightened up. Nothing—yet, she added fiercely. But it *would* happen. It would.

Out of the corner of her eye she caught sight of something glinting outside the window, and suddenly realised that it was the sun shining off a row of cars parked outside the hospital.

She blinked in surprise. It was a beautiful day out there, with a bright blue sky and decorative beds crammed with late summer flowers.

When had that happened?

The last time she remembered looking at the weather it had been a chilly late spring day and she'd been waiting to find out whether Mac had survived the crash.

How had the time passed so fast without her noticing?

On a daily basis, she'd coped with the passing of another shift, another day off, another week's shopping, another month's bills. She'd even accurately tracked the fact that she was now halfway through her pregnancy and carrying an increasingly active child around inside her.

The trouble was, everything seemed to have been happening in a vacuum, totally unconnected to the rest of the world.

She was still a little bemused when she looked around the unit and saw how many changes in occupancy there had been since the first night she'd sat beside Mac's bed. There was only one other person in the department who hadn't either recovered, moved on to another facility for the next stage of their recovery or died.

She looked at each bed in turn, recalling what she knew of their present occupants.

The first one nearest to her was a middle-aged woman who hadn't known she'd had an aneurysm at the base of her brain until it had sprung a leak and she'd collapsed in a coma.

Professor Squires had been able to repair the burst blood vessel and now her family was waiting to see if she was going to recover without any evidence of brain damage after the enormous blood loss.

'How is it going?' she asked the young woman sitting beside the bed. Their facial similarities were strong enough to proclaim her the patient's daughter, and Kara had spoken to her often enough to know that she was struggling to spend time with her mother, while trying to organise three young school-age children on their long summer holidays.

'If you mean life at home, it's chaos,' she said with a grimace. 'My house looks like a bomb dropped in it, and if I don't get the kitchen cleaned up soon I think I'll need to wipe my feet when I come *out* of it rather than go in. It'll take a pick and shovel to find the top of the cooker!'

'What about your mum?' Kara was almost certain the news was better because the woman's mood was completely different today—far more upbeat.

'She opened her eyes!' The woman's face was covered in a huge grin. 'Then she told me I looked dreadful!'

'And you've never been so happy with an insult in your life,' Kara guessed.

'She'll be mortified when I tell her what she said. She's always told us that if we can't say anything nice, we shouldn't say anything at all.'

Kara left her to her knitting, knowing it wouldn't be long before she lost contact with yet another family who had been touched by tragedy. At least it looked as if they were going to survive the ordeal intact.

Next to her was a young man who'd barely reached his twenties.

'Motorbike mad,' his father had said sadly when Kara had struck up a conversation late one night when he'd first arrived in the unit. 'Ever since he was tiny, all he ever wanted to do was race motorbikes. Trouble is, it's so competitive when they're going for sponsorship that some of them push it and take stupid chances. Duncan just didn't stand a chance when someone tried to force their way past on a tight bend.'

He'd shown Kara photos of a lean, fit youngster with a wide happy grin on his mud-splattered face as he cradled his helmet in the crook of one arm and posed on his precious bike.

'A freak accident, they said,' the older man had continued with his eyes swimming with tears. 'He always wore top-of-the-line protective gear and the bikes are only light, but they were all going so fast that they couldn't avoid him. Several of them hit him so hard that they shattered his helmet and drove a shard of it straight into his head.'

Kara shuddered. He'd hardly mentioned the fact that now his poor son also had half a hardware shop holding his various shattered bones together.

Now he was sat beside his son's bed with his head pillowed on his arms. Even in his sleep Kara could see that one hand was holding on tightly to his son's limp hand.

The poor man looked positively grey with exhaustion and the last thing Kara wanted to do was disturb his sleep.

In the next bed was a recent addition. He'd only been here a matter of hours and she didn't know any more about him than the bare details one of his team had given her the last time she'd come out of Mac's room to stretch her legs.

It was difficult to feel sorry for a man who deliberately got behind the wheel of a car, knowing he was very drunk. The damage after his collision with a very large, very solid tree hadn't been helped by the fact he'd forgotten to put his seat belt on. Not only had he gone right through his windscreen, he'd also hit the tree head first.

The amazing thing was that no one else had been injured in his four-mile slalom race towards oblivion.

The people Kara *did* feel sorry for were his wife and family, knowing that they were probably going to lose him in the very near future.

His wife was beside him now, her eyes red and swollen from the tears she'd shed during her vigil. Kara smiled sympathetically, willing to spend a little time with her if she wanted the company, but she looked away, feigning an interest in the various monitor read-outs.

The next man had been a big burly farmer not very long ago.

When he'd gone to his doctor with an insidious nagging ache in his back and a growing tendency to stumble, he'd been sent away with a flea in his ear and instructions not to waste the busy man's time.

He'd been fuelled by desperation when he'd finally made an appointment with a chiropractor, never having been to anyone outside the usual health service channels before.

The evidence the complementary therapist had found within the first few minutes of beginning his initial examination had had the poor farmer in an ambulance on his way to St Augustine's.

At first sight the X-ray evidence had looked like an abscess on the spinal cord—a potentially lethal condition if it burst and spread its poison straight up into the brain, to say nothing of the paralysis it would cause with the damage to the spinal cord itself.

It hadn't been until further tests had been done that the suspected abscess had been revealed as a tumour, one of several metastases from undiagnosed cancer of the prostate.

The professor had operated, Mrs Eland had told Kara, but he'd been scrupulously honest when he'd told the two of them that the operation had only been successful up to a point. It had bought a little time for the two of them to come to terms with what was coming, but it hadn't been able to do anything about the root cause.

'As soon as he's recovered enough to go home, we're going to sell the farm to our neighbour,' she confided over a cup of tea. 'He wants the farmhouse for his son and daughter-in-law to move in when they get married in a few months, and they need the extra acreage if they're going to be able to support the next generation of little mouths.'

'What about your family?' Kara asked, sad that they were going to sell the results of a lifetime of effort.

'Neither of them wanted to work the land,' Mrs Eland said with a small, sad smile. 'Our daughter's a teacher—head of department now—and our son is aiming to be a barrister before he's finished.'

'Where will you live when the farm's gone?'

'There's a little cottage on the edge of the property. It used to be where the cowman lived when we could afford one, but then we had it done up and used it for holiday lets for a couple of years. It'll feel a bit like living in a doll's house after a big rambling farmhouse, but it's big enough for the two of us.'

She was a little wiry woman whose whole body was evidence that she'd spent her life working right beside her husband. There was an innate pride in the way she held herself, knowing she didn't owe the world a thing.

'It's right on the edge of the village, within shouting distance of the people we've known all our married lives—longer for Geoff because he was born there. Then, once we've moved in and got ourselves straight, we've decided we're going to take the long holiday we've always promised ourselves. No point in stinting ourselves now.'

'Good for you,' Kara said quietly, amazed how pragmatic she was about the whole situation. Perhaps it was a result of so many years of working with nature's whim that made her so accepting of what couldn't be changed.

Even after all these months of working for Mac's recovery, she still couldn't countenance losing the man she loved the way this brave woman was.

'We're going to make sure we do it soon, while Geoff's still strong enough to enjoy it,' Mrs Eland added firmly. 'Then we'll have a whole lot more memories to talk about when things start getting bad again.'

Kara was startled when the little woman suddenly reached out and gave her a swift hug.

'You look after yourself,' she murmured. 'It's never wrong to fight for him if he's worth fighting for. I've had thirty-seven wonderful years with Geoff and I wouldn't have missed a single minute, even knowing what's coming.'

Kara felt the burn of threatening tears but she fought them fiercely. She couldn't afford to weaken now or she might never be able to summon up the strength to carry on.

She managed a hug and a smile for the courageous woman and when she saw Mr Eland stirring and reaching across the covers to find his wife's hand she made herself walk on to the next bed.

The youngest patient in the unit was still in his teens. A bright lad studying for exams to get him into medical school, he'd initially ascribed his headaches to too many hours spent bent over his books. It wasn't until he'd felt a growing tingle in one hand and a weakness in the leg on the same side that he'd realised it could be something far more serious.

The surgery to remove the tumour from his brain had been very complex and had taken hours of minutely painstaking effort. Professor Squires hadn't said much yet, but Kara was beginning to be able to read his expression after all this time and she had a feeling that he was quietly optimistic about the outcome.

'Any visitors due today?' Kara asked, leaning against the side of the bed when he smiled a welcome.

'Don't think so,' he said softly, his speech still slightly slurred. 'Brother's got himself a holiday job as a lifeguard—hoping to get some of the girls while I'm out of the way.'

'He doesn't stand a chance when you're around, does he?'

'Nah. I got all the brains in the family as well as all the looks and the charm.'

Kara chuckled. She'd met his brother—an identical twin with exactly the same goals and determination to achieve them. She'd also seen that this sort of rivalry was perfectly normal between the two of them.

'Poor chap, he's going to have another strike against him when you go home. You'll have your operation to talk about and all the girls will be flocking to play Florence Nightingale.'

'You don't think I could persuade Professor Squires to give me another scar in a slightly more interesting place, do you?' he asked wistfully. 'Having girls lining up to inspect my scars would be a lot more exciting if they were below my waist rather than above my neck.'

Kara chuckled. 'No chance,' she said. 'You're dangerous enough with half your head shaved, without having any other advantages. Keep your mind on your studies for a few more years.'

Alison was signalling from the other side of the room that she'd made a cup of tea and Kara nodded, before saying her goodbyes and making her way through the familiar cacophony to the small room just beyond.

'You've come up for a few minutes of fresh air, have you?' she greeted Kara as she joined her. 'I was going to go in and winkle you out if you didn't appear soon.'

'I decided I needed to stretch my legs,' Kara agreed as she went across to join Alison beside the open window.

One of the flowering plants nearby was giving off a beautiful perfume that drifted in to meet them, and when Kara drew in a deep breath she felt her spirits lifting.

'Gorgeous isn't it?' Alison agreed. 'There's been just enough rain this year for the grounds to be at their best.'

'Quite depressing when you think all this will be gone in another month, then we'll start the slow slide into winter,' Kara added.

'Still, at least this autumn will go quickly because there'll be something special to look forward to,' Alison pointed out.

'You mean the baby?' Kara smoothed her hand over the bump that was still largely camouflaged by a lightweight smock-style dress printed with a muted riot of blue and white flowers.

'That and the start of the new millennium,' Alison corrected her. 'If the TV and papers are to be believed, the whole world is going to be having one enormous party.'

'I don't think me and my enormous bump will be in any sort of shape to take part,' Kara said with a chuckle. 'I shall be the size of a hippopotamus by then and longing for the middle of January.'

'Knowing my luck, I shall be on duty,' Alison predicted with a grimace. 'Still, we could have a pact. If we're both here, we'll have to open a bottle of bubbly and toast each other.'

Kara agreed with every appearance of lightheartedness, but inside she dreaded the thought that she might still be visiting Mac then.

With every passing week the chance that he would emerge from the coma would fade, as would the chance that his brain function would be intact. If Mac was still here in the unit when the rest of the world was celebrating the start of the next century, she wouldn't have much to celebrate.

Deliberately cutting off her dismal thoughts, she turned to Alison and asked her about the date she'd been on with one of the SHOs.

'Don't ask,' Alison said with a groan. 'I knew there must be some reason why I had second thoughts as soon as I accepted.'

'What went wrong? I thought he was going to take you out to that rather swish Indian restaurant.'

'Oh, he did. Unfortunately, he didn't realise until we got to the end of the meal that he'd left his wallet at home. And that was after he'd eaten all of his meal and half of mine as well!'

At her disgusted expression, Kara burst out laughing.

'So what happened? Did the two of you have to do the washing-up to pay for the meal?'

'I didn't think of that! I could have walked out and left him to it!' Alison exclaimed. 'As it was, muggins that I am, *I* paid for it.'

'And was it worth paying for?' Kara prompted.

'You mean, rather than having the restaurateur calling for the police?'

'No. I mean, had you enjoyed the meal and the company up till then? Was it a good evening?'

'Actually…' Alison went a bit pink and wouldn't meet Kara's eyes. 'Actually, it was probably the best meal I've had in a very long time. We talked and talked for hours.' Her smile faded by degrees as she went silent.

'But?' Kara prompted. 'I'm sure I heard a "but" in there somewhere.'

'But…he was so embarrassed about forgetting his wallet that even if he fulfils his promise to pay me back I'll probably never hear from him again.'

'Hmm. Tricky. The male ego is such a fragile flower,' Kara agreed, and thought for a minute. 'Hey! I've got it. You could turn the tables on him. You could get in first by inviting him out to a venue of your choice and warn him that *he's* paying this time.'

Alison started off by shaking her head but Kara could see the idea intrigued her.

'Of course,' Kara added sneakily, 'it all depends how much you enjoyed his company the first time whether you really want to see him again.'

Alison grinned and held both hands up in a gesture of surrender. 'I think you've got to know me too well over the last few months. You know exactly which buttons to press, don't you?'

Kara just smiled. Sue had said the same thing just a few days ago.

It was amazing how many times her friend Sue had 'accidentally' turned up to keep Kara company just in time to bump into Mike—as if Kara hadn't guessed what was going on between the two of them.

Still, she'd been able to turn the situation to her own advantage on a couple of occasions, discovering that Mike was only too willing to talk when Sue was there to listen too...

'So, where did you and Mac find out about this applied clinical neurology?' she'd asked, pursuing a previous unfinished conversation.

'Mac probably told you we both went to the same chiropractor when we played rugby during our training?'

'Yes, and it's always struck me as a particularly crazy situation that medical schools often have blood-thirsty rugby teams that regularly break bones and put each other in hospital.'

'Well, it's a collision sport,' Mike had said with a dismissive shrug. 'Anyway, the two of us found this chap—an Australian married to an Irish lass—who started telling us about this applied neurology course he was doing in America.'

'Wow. Talk about international,' Sue had exclaimed.

'That wasn't the half of it,' Mike had said. 'He sent us the information with the news that they were starting a course of seminars in Amsterdam. We signed up for the first one and it completely blew us away. Three days of virtually non-stop lectures from eight in the morning till eight at night, and the guy never had to refer to notes once.'

Just the thought of it boggled Kara's mind.

'We'd never had neurology broken down that way, or put together. You know when you were doing your training you had to learn about brain function?'

Kara and Sue nodded, both pulling faces when they remembered the complexity of the material they'd had to learn before they could pass their exams.

'Well, you probably thought it was bad enough learning the basics such as the anatomy of the brain and the different functions of each area. Imagine what it's like when you have someone standing up there and tracing the neural pathways that directly and indirectly link the stretch receptors in your feet to your brain through the spino - vestibulo - cerebellar - rubro - thalamo - cortico - striato - cortico - rubro - reticulo - spinal feedback loops— among others!'

Kara choked back a gasp of laughter, not certain for a moment whether Mike was joking.

'You're serious?' she demanded. 'That's what I'm firing into each time I stretch Mac's foot?'

'Each gentle stretch does all that work,' Mike confirmed. 'That's why it's so important that you don't do too much. With that many tracts involved in such a simple movement, you can see how easy it would be to overload the system and blow fuses.'

'I'm glad you didn't tell me all that when I started, or I'd have been too terrified to touch him. For heaven's sake *don't* tell me what all the other things are doing to him. I always thought it was as simple as flicking a switch to turn on a light.'

'There are an awful lot of people who still think that way, and too many of them are working in hospital neurology departments,' Mike said darkly. 'But that's my hobby-horse, and I'll ride it for ever once I get up on it.'

'In that case, perhaps you and Sue had better go and leave me to terrify myself with all the things that could go wrong if I squeeze Mac's hand too tightly,' Kara suggested with a wicked grin. 'I know you're only using a visit to Mac as an excuse to meet up without tipping the rest of the staff off that you're seeing each other.'

'I told you she'd see through us,' Sue said, the high colour in her cheeks only marginally hotter than in Mike's.

'And I thought we'd developed subtlety into an art form,' Mike said.

'Subtlety!' Kara hooted. 'The two of you haven't been able to take your eyes off each other since...' Since the wedding, she'd been going to say, but the wedding had never taken place. 'Since the first time you met,' she substituted quickly. 'Still, as it's exactly what Mac and I had in mind when we asked the two of you to stand up for us, I suppose I can't complain if it worked so well.'

'What do you mean—you planned it?' Sue demanded. 'You never said a word to me about any plans.'

'Well, she wouldn't, would she?' Mike said wryly. 'Is this the point where we say thank you?'

'Only if the relationship is really headed where I think it's headed,' Kara said with a smile, watching the way the two of them could hardly stay away from each other.

She watched them exchange a telling glance before Mike took Sue's hand and they turned to face her.

'Actually, I've asked Sue to marry me,' he said, with an endearing touch of shyness.

'And did she accept?' Kara teased.

'Of course I did!' Sue exclaimed, then giggled when she realised that her friend was only ragging her.

'I'm so pleased for you,' Kara said honestly as she gave them both a hug. 'Have you set a date?'

'Well, yes and no,' Sue admitted, looking slightly uncomfortable. 'It all depends on you.'

'On me? Why, for heaven's sake?'

'Because we'd both like you to be there with us, but we didn't know whether you'd rather not in view of Mac.' She gestured towards the silent figure around whom the whole conversation had been flowing for the last half-hour.

'If things had been different, I would have liked Mac to have been my best man,' Mike said honestly. 'But with no precise date for when he'd be fit for the duty…'

'He wouldn't expect the two of you to put your plans on hold, and neither would I,' Kara said firmly, deliberately ignoring a sharp pang of sadness. If things had worked out the way she and Mac had planned, the two of them would have been best man and matron of honour at their friends' wedding.

'Where were you thinking of getting married?'

'At home,' Sue said swiftly. 'We both decided we wanted our families around us, but we don't want one of those overblown affairs that take years to put together.'

'The plan is that you and Sue will go out to find

her a dress. My mother and Sue's mum are organising the reception between them, and we're keeping our fingers crossed for a touch of Indian summer in three weeks' time.'

'Three weeks!' Kara exclaimed. 'Will that be long enough?'

'It will be long enough for what we want,' Sue said firmly, her hand linked with Mike's. 'It's going to be a meeting of a group of family and friends who want to wish us well on our wedding day.'

'Anyone who wants to take photos will be welcome on the understanding that they let us have copies of all the incriminating ones for future blackmail use,' Mike teased, then grew serious.

'Actually, it was you and Mac who made us decide to do it this way,' he admitted quietly. 'We all realise exactly how fickle fate can be, and we decided that it was the marriage that mattered rather than the wedding.'

'You will come, won't you?' Sue pleaded. 'It just wouldn't be right if neither of you were there. Will you be my bridesmaid?'

Kara looked down at her burgeoning waistline and chuckled.

'Sue, this is not the figure of a maid, and as I'm not married I can't be a matron of honour.'

'Oh, but that doesn't matter…'

'I'd rather not be put in the limelight as your attendant,' Kara continued quickly, not giving her friend time to get up a persuasive head of steam. 'But I would be delighted to be with you to wish you well on your special day—from both of us.'

CHAPTER SIX

'I'VE brought you a present,' Sue announced when she joined Kara in Mac's room.

'You shouldn't. It's not my birthday for ages yet,' Kara remonstrated. 'Anyway, you should be buying the last-minute things for your wedding, not things for me.'

'Ah, but this isn't strictly for you,' Sue said with a gleam in her eye. 'I was just idly wandering along, trying to work out if I'd got everything on my list. You know the sort of thing—suspenders and stockings to wear under my dress to drive him mad when he finds out, a sexy nightdress for the first night of the honeymoon...

'Anyway,' she continued airily, as if she hadn't just been her usual outrageous self, 'I found myself outside that gorgeous little shop that does all the baby things, and suddenly my feet wouldn't let me walk past.'

'Sue...' Kara began, not knowing how to tell her friend that she had too much on her mind, with thinking about her friend's wedding and about Mac's slow response to treatment, to contemplate starting to buy things for the baby. Besides, there were still months to go before she was due to deliver.

'Anyway, once I was in there it was just full of the most gorgeous things. And they were so tiny and so perfect I almost started feeling broody myself. Look!'

She tugged a little all-in-one sleeper in fluffy white

stretch towelling out of a suspiciously full-looking carrier bag. 'It hardly looks big enough to cover a baby rabbit, does it? And they had it in all sorts of edible soft pastel shades…aqua, powder blue, sugared almond pink, soft lemon…'

'Sue! You didn't!' Kara exclaimed, but Sue was already busy pulling out one of each colour.

'Well, they were so perfect I just couldn't resist them,' she said with a pout. 'And you've got to start collecting some clothes for the little thing some time or once it arrives it's going to have to stay stark naked until you're fit to go out shopping.'

'But there's still plenty of time,' Kara said, in spite of the fact that Sue obviously wasn't listening. She was far too busy delving into the bag again.

'And look at this,' she demanded, brandishing a handful of brightly coloured objects. 'As an honorary auntie, I reserve the right to be the donor of all the gruesomely noisy toys every child simply must have. The trumpet, the drum, the tinny toy piano—and this!'

She brandished a teething rattle in the air as she passed it over the top of Mac for Kara to take.

Kara's hand froze in mid-air and the rattle fell to the bed.

'Did you see that?' she demanded breathlessly, her eyes fixed frantically on Mac's face. 'Sue, did you see that? He moved. Mac moved.'

Kara's hands were shaking as she reached out to cup his face, terrified that she might have imagined it.

'Mac, can you hear me?' she begged, her voice as shaky as her hands. 'Please, Mac, I saw you move. I *know* I saw you move.'

She waited breathlessly for endless seconds but nothing happened.

'Please, Mac,' she repeated. 'If you can hear me, *please* let me know…'

Out of the corner of her eye she could see Sue shifting uncomfortably from one foot to the other.

'You *must* have seen him,' she said accusingly, her heart pounding in her chest with a mixture of terror and elation. 'He *did* move. When you were passing me the rattle it was almost as if…as if he flinched away from it.

'That's it!' she exclaimed, grabbing the discarded rattle and giving it a single experimental shake by Mac's ear.

As if on command, Mac flinched away from the sound, his pained expression clearly showing his dislike of it.

'Oh, my God,' Sue breathed. 'You were right!'

'Where's Mike?' Kara demanded when she'd gently tried the same test by Mac's other ear and had elicited a similar result. 'Is he free to come and see this? Is it a good sign? Does it mean Mac's starting to wake up?'

'I'll find him,' Sue promised, dropping her shopping in a heap on the floor as she hurried out of the room.

She must have said something on her way out because within seconds every spare member of staff in the unit was crowding round Mac's door.

'What happened, Kara?' demanded Alison, one of the first to arrive. 'Sue said something about Mac moving, or rattling, or something, and then she took off like a greyhound after a rabbit.'

Kara chuckled, halfway between laughter and tears.

Blinking furiously, she tightened her hold on Mac's hand and drew in a steadying breath.

'She was just showing me some things she'd bought for the baby, and when she shook the rattle Mac flinched away from the noise,' she explained succinctly.

'Will he do it again?' someone else called. 'Does it happen every time?'

'I tried it and he did it again, but until Mike's had a look at him I don't want to do it any more in case it's not a good sign.'

'But if it's proof that he can hear something, how can it be bad?' demanded another voice. 'Surely you should do it as often as possible so he gets the idea.'

'He's not a performing monkey,' Kara said sharply, then bit her tongue in dismay. 'I'm sorry. I'm just so wound up about this. I'd love to sit here and watch him respond all day, but first I need to know that the noise of the rattle isn't doing him some harm that's making him flinch away from it. It could be something to do with the frequency of the noise, or the fact that it startled him...anything.' She shrugged helplessly.

'Well, as soon as you know, pass the message on,' Alison demanded with a mock-ferocious wag of her finger. 'We're all waiting for a good excuse to celebrate with you.'

Kara promised to let them know and the room quickly emptied until only Alison was left.

'I'm sorry I jumped down their throats, but—'

'You've got nothing to apologise for,' Alison interrupted. 'You've fought like a tiger for months to help Mac. If that lot haven't realised by now that you're not going to do anything that might put his progress at risk, then they're not the intelligent people I took them for.'

Kara smiled wanly and linked her fingers through Mac's to bring his hand up to her lips, closing her eyes to concentrate on a heartfelt prayer. Please, God, she thought, the words overflowing in a torrent from her brimming heart. Please, God, let this be the first really big step towards his recovery.

The sound of Mike's voice, mingling with Sue's, had her eyes flying open, and they were fixed feverishly on the open door when the two of them appeared.

'So what have the two of you been up to while my back was turned?' Mike teased as he began his usual swift check-over. 'Sue said something about buying that baby of yours some maracas.'

Kara pointed silently at the innocuous-looking object lying on the plain white sheet, her mouth too dry for speech.

'Tell me exactly what happened,' he demanded as he propped one hip on the edge of the bed. 'Exactly.'

Kara swallowed and drew in a shaky breath.

'Sue and I were chatting about her shopping and she was shaking the rattle as she passed it across the bed to me. Out of the corner of my eye I saw Mac flinch but I didn't know what he was reacting to at first. Then I rattled it again, and he turned away again and pulled a face.'

'How many times have you done it to check his response?'

'Once each side, just to check that's what he was reacting to, then nothing until you came and told me what it means,' Kara told him honestly. 'What *does* it mean, Mike? Does it mean he's started hearing me? Does it mean he's waking up at last?'

'For a start, it's confirmation that he's probably been hearing you for some time now.' He raised a hand to prevent her outburst when she would have interrupted. 'Not all the time, because his level of consciousness varies the same way ours does between waking and sleeping. And he's not necessarily understanding everything he's hearing, but this is proof that his brain is not only receiving messages from his ears but is starting to sort out the sounds it likes and those it doesn't.'

'And the movement? The expression on his face?' Kara demanded, afraid to hope for too much after all this time.

'That's a good sign too. It's proof of functioning connections between different areas of the brain.'

'Mike, don't blind us with another long string of words, will you?' Sue warned. 'Once was enough.'

'All right. I won't,' he conceded. 'What I will tell you is that he's ready for more sounds now.'

'What sort of sounds?' Kara was eager to find out what she had to do next. Anything to help bring Mac back to her.

'Crumpling paper, cracking eggshells, the sound of a whisk against a bowl, the click and scrape of cutlery on a plate, sawing a piece of wood, hammering a nail into wood. You could sing to him or play him a tape of nursery rhymes he would have heard as a child. Apart from anything else, it'll be good practice for you for when the baby comes.'

'Normal volume, or starting off softly again?' Kara asked. She was almost certain she already knew the answer, but felt it was important to ask.

'Softly. Everything softly, and the sharper sounds just for a few seconds at a time. And talk about what you're doing at the same time… ''I'm setting the table, now, Mac. Can you hear the knives and forks?'' And so on.'

'How often should I do it? How many times a day? How many different things in a day?' Suddenly she couldn't bear it that everything had to be taken slowly. It was so long since she'd made her promise to be patient, and her patience was starting to wear very thin.

'Ah, Kara, be careful,' Mike warned softly. 'Remember, you mustn't drive the poor horse too fast or too hard just because you've got him to take his first few tottering steps. You're trying to improve the function of Mac's brain first, not just force him to show a reaction to a noise. His reaction to that baby's rattle is a case in point. The sound is probably too fierce at this stage and could overload his system.'

'It's served its purpose, anyway,' Kara conceded with a resigned smile for Sue, waiting patiently on the other side of the bed. 'Just by letting us know that Mac was ready to respond to more sounds, it was worth every penny you spent on it.'

'Glad to be of service,' Sue said with a smart salute and a grin. 'I'll wait a bit longer before I buy the drum and the trumpet, shall I?'

Kara laughed at Mike's confused expression and suggested Sue explained the joke as she escorted him back to where she'd found him.

Finally, the room was peaceful and quiet again, and she settled herself down beside Mac for just a little while longer until it was time to take herself off to bed.

'Oh, Mac, I miss you,' she whispered as she laid her head on his shoulder.

It was an awkward position when he was lying in bed like this and she was sitting on a chair beside him, but it was where she'd always ended up when they were alone together.

Whether they were sitting side by side on the floor in front of the fire, their backs braced against the front of the settee, or lying in each other's arms in bed, her head had always come to rest just there. It was as if the shape of his shoulder and his chest had been specially designed for her head to nestle in beside his jaw.

'The bed is so lonely without you beside me,' she whispered, smoothing her cheek against the angle of his jaw, her hand resting over the steady beat of his heart. 'It's cold and lonely even in the summer, not warm and cosy the way it is when we snuggle up together.'

Her emotions began to get the better of her and she reined them in fiercely. It wouldn't help Mac to recover if she lost control now. She must be strong for him.

'I'm so pleased for you, that you're ready to move on to the next step,' she murmured, a quick mental list of things she would have to remember to bring with her flashing into her mind's eye. 'Don't mind me that I wish your rate of recovery could be as fast as our courtship. Perhaps I should keep some kind of score and make you pay your debts off when you've recovered. How many hugs do you think you owe me now? How many kisses?'

She tilted her head to give him her usual parting kiss, as ever waiting for that missing response.

'Sleep well, my love,' she said, refusing to allow her disappointment to colour her voice. 'I'll see you tomorrow.'

'Tomorrow…' 'My love…' 'Tomorrow…'

The words echoed strangely inside his head and he tried to concentrate, but now that she wasn't holding his hand any more it seemed so much harder.

It was harder to drift off into the darkness, too. More and more she was forcing him to come nearer to the noise and the light and the pain.

Sometimes he fought her, longing to be left alone where everything was so peaceful, but she was stronger than he was and so very determined.

She touched him.

Every day she touched him and sometimes it seemed as if she was intent on waking every nerve in his body until he wished he could scream out for her to stop.

But then she stopped and something inside him cried out for her to continue, just so he could feel her touch again. Something hidden deep inside his brain knew that he shared a special connection with her…that she was the reason he was here. But why? Why?

There were no answers.

There were never any answers.

'Oh, Mac, I wish you could have been there,' Kara said late the following Saturday evening as she settled down to tell him about Sue's and Mike's wedding.

'The weather has been absolutely perfect today. Clear and sunny without being too hot. It meant that lots of the ladies were able to wear summery dresses and hats, just like Sue.'

She'd told him the other day that her friend had decided against wearing a traditional white dress and had chosen a slightly formal-looking summer dress that was the perfect mixture of elegance and prettiness.

The silk fabric was as light as a whisper and the floral print in a mouth-watering mixture of cream and pale apricot meant that she would be able to wear her special dress many times to add to the special memories.

She'd worn a hat rather than a traditional veil and had insisted that Kara buy herself one at the same time on their madcap pre-wedding shopping trip.

Kara glanced down at the smart navy silk dress she was still wearing, stroking a finger over Wedgwood-blue and dove-grey floral sprays which Sue had insisted were the perfect foil for her grey-blue eyes. She hadn't bothered stopping off at her room to change when she returned to the hospital, hurrying straight to Mac's room to tell him all about the events of the day.

She'd told herself it was because she didn't want to waste any time when she would only be getting undressed for bed soon, but perhaps one small corner of her mind was hoping that he would see her in something really flattering if he were to open his eyes tonight.

'I didn't really want to spend a lot of money on a special dress, not the shape I am at the moment, but Sue said the colour and the style really suited me. Then she pointed out that I could always keep it for her to borrow when she and Mike decide to start their f-family.'

She paused and had to swallow hard to get her

voice under control again. She was determined she wasn't going to give in to her misery.

'Anyway, I looked very smart and Sue said some people hadn't even noticed my bulge until I balanced my plate on it.'

She tried to sort through the kaleidoscope of images to choose some to describe to Mac.

Suddenly all she could remember was the look of love Sue and Mike had exchanged when he'd been told he could kiss his new bride.

It had been a lovely informal family wedding, and they'd just looked so happy to be surrounded by all their friends. Sue had been almost floating on air as she'd turned to face the congregation, and if Mike's smile had been any wider…

Suddenly it was all too much and for the first time since Mac's accident Kara buried her face in Mac's warm, naked shoulder and burst into great, wrenching sobs.

'Oh, God, Mac, it's just not f-fair,' she wept, tears streaming down to form a puddle in the hollow of his collarbone. 'It should have been *us* getting m-married. *We* should have been the ones s-sharing that first special kiss and w-walking back down the aisle.'

For long moments she wept as if her heart were breaking as rage and envy and sorrow fought for supremacy inside her.

She'd managed to keep everything under control for so long now, keeping herself as busy as possible so she didn't notice just how long it was that Mac had been lying there helpless.

It had been nearly six months now, and everything she'd read had told her that the longer the situation went on the less likely it was that Mac would ever recover from the trauma.

All the time she'd been rushing backwards and forwards between her job on Obs and Gyn and working with Mac she'd been able to convince herself that it was just a matter of time before he opened his eyes and spoke to her.

In all those days and weeks and months she'd never let herself think about the alternative Professor Squires had tried to make her face—the fact that her part in triggering Mac to take those first fateful breaths might have been the unkindest thing she could have done to him.

In all this time she'd never allowed herself to wonder if he would rather have died gently that day, just slipping away without ever knowing any of the pain he would have to go through on the road to even a partial recovery.

Had she done him any favours if this was as much as his life would ever be?

She'd kept her spirits up all this time in the belief that he would recover fully. What if it had all been one enormous delusion? What if he was never going to recover?

'Hey, hey, none of this,' said a kindly voice. 'I can't have you drowning my patients.'

A large wad of paper hankies was pressed into her clenched fist and gentle hands lifted her out of her soggy huddle until she was upright on her seat again.

She mopped ineffectually at her face but there were still so many tears streaming from her eyes that she could barely focus on the figure bending over her.

'Kara, dear, you're going to make yourself ill if

you carry on like this,' he said, and she suddenly recognised the voice. It was Professor Squires.

'Oh, P-Professor. I'm s-sorry. I d-didn't want to c-cry, but…' She shook her head, unable to continue.

'I expect you've done a great deal of crying over the last few months,' he said gently. 'It's only natural after all the—'

'N-no…' she wailed. 'I mustn't. If I c-cry then I can't be s-strong for M-Mac. I've g-got to be s-strong—'

'Nonsense,' he interrupted, with not a hint of his usual professorial tones. 'We all need to cry sometimes even if it's only to prove we're human.'

His kindly smile robbed her of her tenuous hold on her tears and the floodgates opened again.

For interminable minutes she howled wordlessly as all the pain of the past and the fears of the unknown future rose up before her eyes.

It was a long time before the flood began to abate and she realised that the eminent professor had been standing there patiently with one arm around her shoulders while she cried her heart out against the front of his impeccable suit jacket.

'Oh, I'm so sorry,' she said breathlessly as she dabbed at the enormous damp patch she'd put on the expensive fabric. 'I didn't mean to—'

'Shh.' He stilled her hand. 'I'm only glad I could be of some help, even if it was only as a sponge.'

The unexpected joke curved the corners of her mouth upwards.

'That's better. Now, how about telling me what that was all about—or shall I guess?'

He grabbed a spare chair and swung it round to

straddle it, his arms folded across the back as if he had all the time in the world to listen.

'Going on the evidence in front of me—one very smart dress and a matching hat on top of the cabinet there—I'd say you've just come back from a certain wedding and were feeling particularly depressed.'

'It's so stupid to cry now,' she said after a ferocious blow of her nose, unable to deny a word of his supposition. 'It's been months since the accident happened and even then I didn't cry.'

'In which case, I would say this little jag was well overdue. Especially in the light of that high spot the other day when Mac reacted to the rattle. I don't mind telling you that you've achieved far more than I ever expected.'

'How much did you expect?' Kara asked bluntly, suddenly needing to know. There would be no more sticking her head in the sand from now on. It obviously didn't do anyone any good.

'Honestly?' he challenged, and she nodded.

'I told you at the time that it might be better just to let Mac go, and that advice was based on years of experience of seeing patients in apparently identical situations. In spite of that weak gag reflex you demonstrated, when I disconnected the ventilator and he made no effort to breathe it was no more than I expected.'

'But then he took that first breath.' Kara relived the surge of relief all over again, the knowledge that Mac was still alive.

'And I was sorry,' he admitted. 'And I had severe reservations about what you and Mike were trying to do. I couldn't really see that it could ever be enough to help.'

'But it *has* helped,' Kara said.

'Yes, it has. Not only is Mac still alive, but he's actually been improving from month to month—enough for me to do a bit of research of my own into this applied clinical neurology. If you'd asked me to lay odds on his recovery six months ago, I wouldn't have given you—or him—a chance. Now…' He gestured upwards with both hands. 'The sky seems to be the limit, and I'd dearly like to send every one of my team to follow the same course Mac and Mike have done.'

'Is that so impossible, if the benefits to your patients are so great?'

'If I had the finances…' he said with a grimace. 'As it is, I've been picking Mike's brain for months now and gradually revising the methods we've been using within the department. After the things I've seen coming out of this methodology—and witnessing your own dedication—if you were to ask me *now* to lay odds on Mac's chances of recovery, I'd put my money on you winning like a shot.'

'I don't know whether you're just exaggerating to lift my spirits, but if you say any more you're going to start me crying again,' Kara said, her voice sounding as if she had a heavy cold with all the congestion in her nose.

'God forbid,' he said fervently, straightening up out of the chair and returning it to its former place against the wall. 'If my jacket shrinks from all this salt water, my wife is going to put me on a diet.'

Kara gave a watery chuckle and found it easier than she expected to smile as the eminent man waved on his way out of the room.

*   *   *

'Antenatal clinic today,' Sue reminded Kara as they made their way across to the obs and gyn department together.

Sue had travelled in with Mike this morning from their new flat a couple of miles the other side of town, and had come to Kara's room to beg a cup of tea before they were both due on duty.

'Thanks for the reminder. I knew I was due to take the clinic this afternoon but I'd actually forgotten all about my part in it,' Kara said with a grimace. Sue seemed to be better than she was at remembering when her appointments were. 'I'd probably have remembered when I saw my name on the list in among the rest—at least in time not to call it out and expect someone to come forward for weighing and so on.'

'Idiot!' Sue chuckled. 'Next, you'll be asking yourself all the usual questions and waiting for an answer. Hop up onto the scales for me, please. How have you been, dear? Have your ankles been swelling? Is your ring getting too tight? Have you brought your urine sample with you?'

'I'm not that bad,' Kara objected. 'I haven't missed a single appointment and everything's going well—absolutely textbook case, I am.'

'Hmm. *I* still think you're underweight. You've never really regained all you lost after Mac's accident. Anyway, be that as it may, it really is about time you started getting yourself organised for that little one's arrival,' she pointed out quietly. 'I can understand that you're very preoccupied with Mac, but at some point the baby is going to have to become your first priority.'

Kara felt a pang of guilt.

'I know,' she admitted with a sigh. 'I think you've

bought more things for it than I have so far. Still, I'll have six whole weeks of maternity leave before it's due to catch up on everything.'

'Everything?' Sue prompted. 'Have you even *started* looking for alternative accommodation?'

'Accommodation?' Kara froze. 'But why would I be needing—? Oh, God. I hadn't thought…'

'Exactly. You know as well as I do that there's no provision for mother and baby in the nurses' block,' Sue reminded her. 'You'll have to move out when the baby arrives, and it would be a great deal easier to move before. Mike and I would be willing to do all the lifting, and he's volunteered the car for the things you need transported.'

'Thanks. But…' She was still stunned. How could she not have realised that she wasn't going to be able to stay where she was? It was so convenient just to be able to buzz backwards and forwards between Neurology, Obs and Gyn and her room, having long ago given up the tiny flat she and Mac had shared.

She'd actually thought far enough ahead to make enquiries about the possibility of a place for the baby in the hospital staff crèche, ready for when she went back to work at the end of her maternity leave.

Even if Mac were to come out of the coma today, it would probably be many months before he was fit enough to return to work—if ever.

His medical insurance benefits, as well as the money his car insurance company had obtained on his behalf, would take care of *his* immediate care, but as they hadn't had a chance to marry, she wouldn't automatically be covered and would need to earn a living for her child and herself.

She hadn't even considered the fact that she would be homeless long before then.

What sort of place would she be able to afford on a nurse's salary? She didn't want anything damp and dingy, not when she would be bringing a new baby home.

The first half of her shift was spent up in the obs and gyn department, but every time she stopped thinking about a patient her brain was elsewhere, worrying about the new problems Sue had pointed out.

By the time the first ladies were due in the antenatal clinic she hadn't found a single solution. All she'd achieved was to raise her own blood pressure and give herself the start of a thumping headache.

It wasn't that she was incapable of sorting her life out—far from it. Before she'd met Mac she'd been virtually on her own since before her parents died, and had managed perfectly well.

But life had been simpler then. There were too many variables to factor in now: Mac's recovery and the number of hours she was devoting to trying to achieve it; her own health while the pregnancy progressed; the impending arrival of a baby totally dependant on her for every aspect of its health and welfare... The list seemed to go on and on.

Her worries sent her thoughts off into new directions as she spoke to each expectant mother. Their conversations seemed to have a new relevance for her now that she was concentrating on that aspect of her own life.

She wasn't so much concerned with the problems suffered by those having their second and subsequent children. At this rate it was unlikely to be a situation she was ever going to experience.

It was the working mothers and their comments about the problems encountered during first-time pregnancies that suddenly seemed to hit home.

Thank goodness she wasn't going to suffer the illegal aggravation of one young woman whose boss was trying to force her into resigning. He was sure that it was a cast-iron way out of having to allow her to take maternity leave with a guaranteed job to return to.

Kara hadn't realised until today that she had addresses she could hand out where worried mums-to-be could go for advice.

The problems surrounding single mums were a growing problem with the year-on-year drop in the rate of marriages, and created their own tensions. Not least was the worry about finding someone suitable and affordable to take care of the child while Mum went back to work.

'I'll have it easier than most,' Kara pointed out to Sue as they tidied away the supplies at the end of the clinic. 'I'll have a good job to return to at the end of my maternity leave, and somewhere safe and reliable for the baby to stay. Once I find myself a little flat, everything should fall into place quite easily.'

'You think so?' Sue said doubtfully. 'What about the times when the baby cries all night and you haven't had any sleep? What if he or she is ill? If you're on your own, there's no one to share the load.'

'Well, there's not a lot I can do about that, is there?' Kara snapped, hating the way her friend had so easily poked holes in the fragile fabric of her romanticised scenario. 'I can hardly ask Mac to take a turn at walking the baby, can I?'

Sue was silent for the rest of the journey back to

Kara's room and she was feeling very guilty for the way she'd snapped at her friend. It wasn't Sue's fault that she was right.

'I'm sorry,' Kara said as soon as the door closed behind them. 'I'm a bad-tempered witch at the moment and I wouldn't blame you if you just washed your hands of me. I'm sure Mike is far better company.'

'Different, not better,' Sue corrected loyally, and gave her hand a squeeze, before dropping gratefully onto the end of the bed and kicking her shoes off.

'Look, Kara, I know it seems as if I'm harping on about the mess you could face in a few weeks, but it's just because I'm worried about you. Mac needs you as much as ever, you're far too professional to give anything less than one hundred per cent to your job, and when the baby comes... You're healthy at the moment but is there going to be anything left of you if you're being pulled in three different directions all the time?'

CHAPTER SEVEN

'HEY, Kara, did you hear about that patient in the ophthalmology department?' Sue demanded as she dashed into Obs and Gyn with just minutes to spare before the start of her shift.

Kara could remember when her friend used to arrive with half an hour to spare, but she and Mike must be putting that time to some other use these days. Whatever it was, it was certainly putting roses in Sue's cheeks and she'd never seen such a bounce in Mike's stride.

The nasty little green-eyed monster started to raise his ugly head but Kara flattened him swiftly. She was glad that her friends were happy and wouldn't allow jealousy to sour their relationship.

'What patient was that?' she responded, patiently holding the extra mug of tea she'd made for Sue while her friend dragged off her outer layers.

October had arrived with a series of gales and it didn't look as if anything was going to change in a hurry. At this rate, it was going to be a very long dreary winter.

'Mike was telling me last night. Oh, thanks.' She gulped down nearly half of the tea, her eyes closed in ecstasy. 'I needed that. We had to park the car at the other end of the car park today and the wind was like a knife.'

'The patient in Ophthalmology?' Kara prompted

with a wry grin, certain that Sue was growing more scatterbrained by the day.

'Oh, yes. Apparently she's been more or less a regular attendee over the last ten years or so because she couldn't see anything out of one eye even though there was apparently no organic reason for it. The problem had been labelled macular degeneration, for the lack of any other diagnosis.'

She was obviously excited by the tale she was telling because she was waving her mug of tea all over the place. Luckily it was more than half-empty now.

'Anyway,' she continued, 'Mike saw her for her last appointment soon after he started at St Augustine's, and discovered that she actually had some slight peripheral vision.'

'So?'

'So when he examined her more closely he found out that one eye, the blind one, wasn't moving at the same time as the other one, and because this would have sent a double image to the brain and confused it, it had just switched itself off.'

'I didn't know they could do that,' Kara exclaimed in amazement, utterly captivated by the unfolding tale.

'Neither did I,' Sue admitted. 'Anyway, he started stimulating the ocular muscles from other areas of the body, particularly her hands and feet—the same way he's been doing with Mac. Then he gave her special eye exercises to help unlock the peripheral ocular muscles so her eyes could begin working together again.'

'And?' Kara prompted when Sue paused to draw breath. 'I take it from your grin that there's a happy ending to this story?'

'She came back in for another appointment with Mike yesterday afternoon and she can see again with that eye!'

'Really! How much? Just shadows, or what?' Kara was amazed.

'She can now read the newspaper with the eye that used to be blind, and her husband said she hasn't stopped smiling for weeks.'

'Wow! What's Mike's next trick? Walking on water?' Kara teased.

'Actually, I think he was just as delighted as the woman was. He was telling me all about it, but I can't understand enough. He didn't say it, but I think he really needed to share his success with Mac, the way they have ever since they started the course together.'

Kara nodded. The knowledge that Mike might never be able to have such a conversation with Mac hurt.

'So, who *can* he talk to?'

'In the end he got in contact with the chiropractor who first told him about Professor Carrick's course and told him all about it. Apparently, the chiropractor's had a number of similar cases and Mike's invited him over for a meal with us at the weekend so they can pick each other's brains. Apparently there are still so few medics able to do this new stuff that the only people Mike can talk to about it are the chiropractors who have already completed the course.'

'Well, when you see him, will you give him my everlasting thanks for persuading Mac and Mike to get in contact with Professor Carrick? If he hadn't…' She shook her head.

If Mike and Mac hadn't done the applied clinical neurology course, and if Mac hadn't told her about the marvellous things he'd started achieving with it, she wouldn't have known who to call on to help Mac after his accident.

Without the application of that specific clinical neurology methodology, Mac would probably be in a permanent vegetative state by now—if he was still alive.

She's here again…at last.

It seems so long since I heard her voice that I was beginning to think I'd imagined her.

It's a soft voice. Warm and gentle and persuasive, like her hands when she strokes them all over my body.

She kneads the muscles and lifts each limb, pushing and pulling in all directions. I know she finds it hard because I can hear it in her voice. If only there was some way I could help…

She's been singing to me. Sweet, simple songs about black sheep and owls and pussycats that make me feel…good. Safe and protected somehow.

It's strange, though. I don't know her songs, but somewhere, deep in the darkness, it's as if I knew them once, a long time ago.

It's the same with the other noises…the rustling and crackling and tapping. They're new, but also very familiar, as are the words that accompany them.

'Crack the egg,' she said, and suddenly, when I heard the sound, I knew what she meant. There was a picture inside my head.

She talks all the time now, and instead of wanting to drift back into the darkness I can't help trying to follow what she's saying.

'Love you,' she says and I can feel it filling me up somewhere inside.

Other words aren't so clear. They almost seem to bypass thoughts and go straight to feelings. They seem to make every nerve wake up, as if waiting for something to happen. Blood flows faster and lungs work harder. It's as if life is trying to take over inside...inside where I'm trapped behind the impenetrable wall of endless greyness.

'Mr and Mrs Lidyatt, would you like to come through?' Kara invited, dreading the next few minutes.

At least this part of the job would be done by the obstetrician. All she would have to do was stand by to offer what comfort she could.

Although how she could offer comfort to the woman when she was standing here showing the signs of a healthy seven-month pregnancy while the poor woman—

'If you remember,' the obstetrician began, cutting through Kara's thoughts and drawing her attention back to the waiting parents, 'we weren't very happy with baby's rate of growth at your check-up a couple of days ago. We took some extra blood and another urine sample to run some tests and we organised for you to come in for an extra ultrasound.'

'That's right. I told Sister here that the baby hadn't been moving about as much since my last visit to the antenatal clinic and wondered if it was because I wasn't eating the right things to give him energy.'

'I'm afraid it's nothing like that,' the obstetrician said gently. 'I'm sorry, but we can't find a pulse for the baby any more. It seems that some time since your last ultrasound the baby's simply died.'

Kara was glad her colleague had carefully avoided using the emotive term 'missed abortion' for the condition he'd diagnosed.

It didn't happen very often, especially this late in a pregnancy, and Kara could only try to imagine how devastated the sobbing woman was feeling.

The first thing *she* had done when she'd discovered the reason for the child's lack of movement had been to give in to her own blind panic.

It had only taken a shaky minute or two to persuade the sympathetic ultrasound technician to do an extra check to make sure that her own baby's heart was still beating away inside her.

Somehow that reassurance only made her feel more guilty now as she offered tea and sympathy. Soon she would have to give as much of an explanation as the poor woman could cope with about the immediate course of events.

'When did it die? *Why* did it die?' demanded the distraught father.

'It could have been at any time in the last four weeks because we know the heartbeat was normal at that antenatal visit. As for why... We may discover that when the foetus is delivered, but most times we never find out what caused it.'

'But if you don't know why it happened, how can you stop it happening again?'

'It's a very rare occurrence—I can't quote exact statistics without looking them up—but ever since I started my training as a doctor, I've never known anyone who had it happen a second time.'

It was small enough consolation for the shocked

and grieving parents to take with them. As Kara escorted them through to one of the newly refurbished side rooms off to one side of the ward, she hoped they never realised the careful way the obstetrician's reassurance had been worded. After such a disastrous event, they would need all their courage to try again for the family they wanted.

In the meantime, because she was well beyond the twenty-eight-week gestational age limit, the poor woman was going to have to go through the miseries of an induced labour, knowing at the outset that none of her pain was going to give her a live baby to love.

The atmosphere in the room was fraught as Kara completed all the preparations, the drip-stand looking strangely ominous when usually it was more of a harbinger of help.

With the danger of dead foetus syndrome hanging over the proceedings, Kara had to stay with the unhappy couple once the oxytocin drip was started. It was hard enough for them to know that they'd lost their baby. Kara was glad that they didn't also know about the possibility that, as a result of carrying her dead baby around inside her, the mother was in danger of suffering from massive bleeding when the delivery finally occurred.

As it was, part of the placenta didn't come away properly and Francesca Lidyatt needed a rapid trip up to Theatre for curettage to remove the remaining fragments.

This was one time that Kara was glad they had the option of keeping a maternity patient in an individual room at St Augustine's. She'd heard horror stories from other hospitals about women trying to come to terms with the tragedy of a stillbirth while surrounded by a ward full of healthy babies.

When her patient came back from Theatre, Kara settled her in a room where there was no possibility of the couple even hearing a baby's cry, let alone seeing one.

'It was a boy,' Francesca Lidyatt murmured, obviously forgetting that Kara already knew. Her husband left the room to stretch his legs for a few minutes. It had been hours since he'd left her side and his face was every bit as grey and drained as hers.

Kara's heart nearly broke at the misery in the woman's voice. She'd tried to imagine how she would feel if it had been her baby who had died, but the concept was too unthinkable, too unbearable.

The life growing inside her was such a precious part of the love she and Mac had shared that if anything happened to it, it would be like losing all contact with the Mac she'd known all over again.

But she hadn't lost Mac. One day he *would* recover. And she wasn't going to lose his baby.

'He was beautiful,' Mrs Lidyatt murmured softly, with silent tears rolling down her face. 'When you let us hold him after he was born, he was so beautiful. Absolutely perfect with not a single mark on him anywhere. He just looked as if he was asleep.'

There was a wounded expression in her eyes as she looked at Kara.

'He didn't deserve to die,' she said, her hands plucking agitatedly at the sheet covering her. 'He'd never done anything wrong and we wanted him so much. We would have loved him even if he hadn't been so perfect.'

'Of course you would,' Kara agreed soothingly as

she reached for the box of paper hankies. 'You'd have loved him because he was yours.'

'We've been planning for him ever since we got married, you know,' she said tearfully. 'The house is big enough for a family and there's a garden.'

Kara wanted to tell the poor woman that she was sure, when they finally had their family, that she and her husband were going to be wonderful parents. But it was too soon to mention the idea of another baby when she was still grieving over the one she had lost.

Mr Lidyatt returned at the same time as Kara's shift ended and she was able to make her farewells to both of them. Provided there were no complications overnight, it was possible that both of them would be long gone by the time Kara started her next shift.

'Oh, Mac, she was so distraught,' Kara said later, taking a few minutes to unburden herself before she started her usual round of exercises and neurological stimulation.

'I couldn't help thinking how I would feel if I lost our baby. It's almost worse, letting myself think about it, because I know about so many of the things that can go wrong.'

It was the same with Mac's situation.

She'd always intended specialising in obstetrics and gynaecology and had therefore had little to do with the long-term care of coma patients.

She now knew more than she'd ever wanted to know about the care and treatment of someone with a severe neurological injury, and far too much about their painfully slow recovery.

The fact that Mac had suffered very little from any of the pitfalls of prolonged immobility—her attention to detail had kept him free of any bedsores and his lungs had remained largely clear—didn't minimise his admittedly poor prognosis.

His mobilisation exercises completed, Kara settled down to the new set of tasks Mike had given her only yesterday.

'Our memory works on lots of different levels,' he'd explained. 'There are the everyday things we do, such as making a cup of tea or changing gear in a car. We don't have to think about them in detail each time because we've done them over and over until it's built into a certain level of our brain called our working memory.'

'Would that include things such as shaving and brushing teeth?' Kara asked, suddenly remembering something she'd been reading in one of Mac's books.

'Exactly. And it's stored in our memory a bit like a back-up copy of a file in a computer.'

'Don't try to confuse me with high-tech stuff,' Kara interjected quickly. 'I don't know a great deal about how computers work.'

'To put it simply, like a computer, your brain keeps a duplicate copy of things you need to use a lot. That means that, if the information is lost from one area, you can actually call it up from the copy and ''learn'' it all over again.'

'So what does that mean for Mac? What background information does he need to learn again?'

'At this level, just the most basic things that have been part of his system for a long time—like the shaving you suggested. You'll need to talk to him as you take him through it in stages—putting the shaving soap on his face, putting the razor in his hand and stroking it over his chin.'

'Won't that be dangerous, letting him hold a razor?'

'For your purposes, you could shave him first then leave the blade out while you get him to copy what you've done. Talk to him all the time, though, to help his brain locate the background copy of the information you want him to recall. You'll be reinforcing it on many levels—the sensation of touch on his face, the fact that he's holding the razor in his hand, the familiar series of movements, and all of it accompanied by the words, telling him what's happening.'

Today was the first time that she would be doing this, and she'd decided to start with simple tasks that Mac must have been doing since he was a small child.

'Time to wash your face, Mac,' she said clearly, taking both of his hands in hers and squeezing his facecloth out in the bowl of warm water. 'Can you feel how warm it is on your skin, Mac? Does it feel good?'

It was awkward, leaning forward with the increasing bulk of her pregnancy getting in the way, so she hitched one hip up onto the bed.

'The flannel's got a nice soft nubbly texture, hasn't it? Shall we rub it over your forehead and down your nose? I think you're going to be delighted when you see what a good job they made of setting that break for you,' she commented in a brief aside. 'It's beautifully straight with not a sign of the old bump and wiggle in the middle. Very aristocratic now,' she added with a chuckle.

'Can you feel the way the cloth is rasping over the new stubble on your cheeks?' she added as she continued her task. 'It sounds as if you'll need a shave soon.'

She had a sudden memory of the first time Mac had kissed her and the way her skin had reddened after its impassioned contact with a day's worth of stubble.

Mac had apologised profusely and made a point after that of shaving twice a day to save her complexion.

'Do you remember that?' Kara said after a quick glance to make certain that the door was closed. She had the blade-less razor clasped in Mac's hand and surrounded by her own now. 'Several times you forgot and grabbed me as soon as you closed the front door, but as soon as you started kissing me you'd lift me up and carry me into the bathroom.'

She had finally understood Queen Victoria's penchant for watching Prince Albert shaving as she'd watched Mac. And it wasn't just the knowledge of what was going to happen between them as soon as he'd finished.

'And then you told me it was my duty to help you make certain that you'd done the job properly.'

She shivered when she remembered some of the tender areas he'd insisted on kissing, just so she could confirm that his face was completely smooth. The rising sensation of heat in her cheeks was almost as embarrassing as her memories, but while she was spending so much of her time talking to Mac and touching him it was hard not to think about the way they'd been together.

It didn't help her equilibrium when Mac's results showed that her conversations designed to stimulate his more basic male responses were having a measurable effect on him. She could hardly stop doing something that was helping his brain to recover vital functions just because it was getting her all hot and bothered.

If he recovered—*when* he finally recovered, she corrected quickly—she would have to make certain he knew exactly what she'd had to go through for him. Thank goodness Mike had become such a good friend or she might never recover from the embarrassment of some of their conversations.

There is something missing.

Sometimes the knowledge seems to be just a heartbeat away and sometimes it is lost in the depths of the darkness that always hovers in the background.

She is here, but who is she? Why is she here? Why does it feel as if her presence is so important?

Every time she comes it is as if I have been waiting for her and every time it seems as if there is a special connection made between the two of us.

Always there is so much to concentrate on that I grow tired and, as if she has heard my thoughts, she stops what she is doing and just holds my hand or lays her head on my shoulder.

She makes the connection that makes it possible for me to continue striving for…what?

There are images in my head. Images that she has put there of the two of us…together.

The thought of us together feels right, especially when the images move on as her voice describes two figures with water streaming down over them.

The images stir something that feels good, something that makes every cell in my body feel alive… If only I knew who she was and why she wants me to picture us this way.

*   *   *

'Hi, Joanne. How is everybody?' Kara asked as she made her way into the department.

She'd been glad to find out that she would be on early shift this morning and would finish at three this afternoon, but when the day arrived it had left far too many hours between the end of her shift and the time when the department would grow quiet with the approach of night.

Today was special for reasons she didn't want to share with anyone other than Mac. Only he would know the reason behind what she had planned for later this evening.

Sue had invited her to share a meal with Mike and herself at their home, but Kara had made her excuses. Now she was wishing she'd accepted. Nerves already had her hands trembling.

'Same old, same old,' Joanne replied, obviously ready for a few minutes' chat.

'Anybody new?'

'We will have, later this evening. There was an accident on the outskirts of the town earlier today and we're going to have one of the victims coming here because there aren't any paediatric beds free. He's only fifteen.'

'What happened? What sort of injuries?'

'Apparently he cycled out to visit a friend, and when he went to set off home he discovered someone had stolen the lights off his bike. There were street-lights and he was wearing reflective gear so he thought he could get away with cycling home without cycle lights.'

'He wasn't knocked down by a motorist?' Kara demanded, horrified.

'No. He was going downhill, less than half a mile

from his home, when he ploughed straight into an unlit skip parked on the road. He was probably going close to thirty miles an hour.'

'Spinal injuries?' Kara could imagine that such a violent collision could have whiplashed his neck so badly that he'd ended up with a broken neck.

'Don't know yet. All we've heard is that he went head first into the steel frame of the skip and he's in surgery while they try to sort out a depressed skull fracture.'

Kara winced and wondered what the young lad's chances were of recovering. She knew that there was no point in asking yet. It would probably be days, if not weeks or months, before anyone had any idea, if Mac's progress was any guide.

'Still, balancing that, we've got Mr Weaver recovering nicely after his surgery,' Joanne volunteered. 'He came round while his wife was sitting beside him and nearly made her jump out of her skin.'

Kara had spoken to Mrs Weaver while she'd been waiting for her husband's post-operative anaesthesia to wear off. Professor Squires had spent several hours removing a cancerous tumour from the man's brain and he'd been optimistic that he'd been able to do the removal without compromising his function.

Now Joanne was confirming that the patient had regained consciousness.

'Is he lucid? Orientated?'

'Not only that, he asked his wife if she'd remembered to feed his ornamental fish before she came to visit,' Joanne said with a laugh.

'How about the rest of them? Mrs Frazer?' Kara knew she was making conversation for the sake of it, but she wasn't asking anything she didn't want to know. It just wasn't important that she asked it *now*.

'She's stabilised nicely, and we'll probably be moving her out onto a normal ward tomorrow morning. She's obviously lost a lot of function on her left side after the stroke, but physio should be able to help to a certain degree. Ditto with Mr Lao. Depending on what sort of night he has, he'll be transferred to the men's ward sometime tomorrow, too.'

'So you'll have empty beds for a change?' Kara said in surprise. It was almost unheard-of with the shortage of specialist nurses.

'Unlikely, if we're starting to take the overflow from Paediatrics. Also, we're starting to get the first wave of the winter flu victims. It would only take a couple of elderly patients to go down with respiratory arrest and we'd be full to bursting in the space of an hour.'

'I'll keep my fingers crossed.' Kara took her first step towards Mac's room. 'Perhaps I'll see you later on this evening?'

'I could bring you in a cup of tea or coffee in a little while, if you like,' Joanne offered.

The thought of Joanne walking into Mac's room without warning made Kara freeze in her tracks.

'Uh, no. No, thanks, Joanne,' she floundered. 'I'd rather wait until I come out to stretch my legs when I've finished Mac's mobilisation and treatment.'

'Anything special on the cards for tonight? Some new music or a new game to play?' Joanne suggested. 'You'll probably be able to hear fireworks going off on that side of the hospital. They've put the display in the grounds round there so the children's department will get a good view.'

'Um, well, I thought I'd just do more of the same tonight,' Kara said lamely. 'You know, trying to get Mac to remember by telling him about things from his past.'

Joanne nodded. She knew what Mike had been telling Kara to do and, having been one of Mac's original carers, had taken the trouble to keep up with each stage of his slow progress.

Guilt that she wasn't being totally honest gripped Kara, but as there was no way she was going to tell anyone what she had planned for tonight, she hurried to make her escape.

'Hello, Mac,' she said as she let herself into the room. She paused a moment to make sure the door was properly closed, then she switched off the main light and pulled down the little blind over the glass observation panel. She wished she had the nerve to lock the door, but common sense prevented her from doing it.

Mac hadn't had any sort of seizure since he'd been moved into this room, but if anything went wrong with him she would never forgive herself if staff couldn't gain access to the room to help him.

She turned to face him and, just for once, stood and looked at him as if she were seeing him for the first time.

There was a single light switched on over the head of his bed, outlining him as if he were under a spotlight. For the first time she noticed that there seemed to be silvery highlights in his dark hair and she suddenly realised that the trauma of the last seven months had brought the start of grey to his temples.

He was only thirty-two years old—wouldn't be

thirty-three until February—but this was evidence of the toll that had been paid by his body.

It had been a long time since he'd moved a single muscle voluntarily, and she'd done her best to keep his body limber, but it was still obvious that he'd lost much of his muscle bulk.

He'd never been a muscle-bound hulk and she wouldn't have wanted him to be, but it would take many weeks before he would be strong enough to walk unaided even if he were to wake today.

Anyway, even as thin as he was, there was something that called out to her. Perhaps it was something in her own brain that appreciated his long, lean symmetry, something that responded to the width of his shoulders, the slenderness of his hips and the length of his legs.

She'd always been fascinated by the broad wedge of silky dark hair that arrowed towards his flat waist, and even as she looked at it her fingers tingled with the memory of how it felt to stroke it. It was a good thing that the plain white hospital sheet was draped modestly across him, at least up to his waist, but it didn't wipe the image of his naked body from her mind.

She smiled when she realised that just standing there, admiring him, had her heart beating faster, and she knew it was time to put her plan into action.

'Hello, Mac,' she murmured again as she bent over him to give him a lingering kiss. 'I hope you're ready to help me celebrate my birthday.'

CHAPTER EIGHT

KARA knew that it was too much to hope that Mac would respond to her kiss or her words, but before she could continue there was a series of sharp bangs outside the window that announced the start of the firework display.

'Can you hear that, Mac?' she asked, almost collapsing onto the chair beside the bed her legs were so shaky. 'It's Bonfire Night again. Bonfire night and my birthday, so I'm catching up on you by a year.'

There was another group of sharp cracks outside, accompanied by bright, multicoloured flashes.

With the light in the room so low, the flashes from the fireworks lit it up as bright as day for whole seconds at a time, then faded, leaving it seeming darker than ever.

Kara swallowed. If she didn't do it now, while she had the perfect accompaniment, she'd probably never get the courage.

'Mac, do you remember taking me to the firework display last year?' she began, linking her fingers through one of his hands and bringing it up to her lips to kiss each knuckle. 'You said it was going the be the start of the most explosive birthday in the world.'

She began to run the fingers of her free hand over the contours of his face, loving him just as much now as she ever had. It had frustrated her sometimes that— typical male—he'd often fallen sound asleep when she'd been ready to talk, but she'd always been able to distract herself by softly exploring his sleeping body.

He looked as if he were just sleeping now, as if all she had to do was tease him, or tickle him, or kiss him, and he would wake and stretch like a lazy lion.

'We were invited to join some of the others for a meal afterwards to help me celebrate my birthday, but you said you'd already booked something.'

She chuckled as she ran her fingers through the silky wedge of hair on his chest then tugged gently.

'I should have remembered that you were Scottish,' she teased. 'When you said you'd booked something, I thought you meant you were taking me to a posh restaurant or something. When we went back to the flat I thought it was so that I could change into something dressier.'

She closed her eyes, remembering the scene that had met her when he'd unlocked the door.

'I didn't know how you'd managed to get back to arrange it, but you'd set up a low table in front of the fire with cutlery and flowers and candles all ready for lighting. And in the fridge was a meal all ready to heat up in the microwave.'

She'd tried to tell him how much his gesture had meant to her but, of course, he'd already known. He'd remembered what she'd told him in the early days of their relationship about the fact that her elderly parents hadn't really wanted the bother of strangers' children underfoot for birthday parties.

He'd remembered, and all those months later he'd found a way to make her birthday special for the first time in her life.

'And it only got better when you gave me my present,' she continued, hearing the husky note that had crept into her voice. 'You wouldn't let me help you clear the table away, and when you came back you turned the lights off so the room was only lit by the fire.

'It was burning brightly as we sat with our backs against the settee, and the flames were reflecting in your eyes when you handed me a parcel wrapped in scarlet and tied with golden streamers.'

He'd groaned when she'd started to unwrap it carefully, wanting to prolong the precious moment.

'"You're killing me, being so slow," you complained, and tried to make me rip it open,' she reminded him with a grin, then had to bite her lip when it started to quiver.

'Oh, Mac, I don't know if I ever managed to tell you just how much I loved your present. I'd never owned anything so sexy and so beautiful.'

And he'd made her feel beautiful when he'd insisted on helping her to model the set of deep scarlet silk and lace lingerie for him.

Explosive had been a good word to describe that night, and she'd felt like a whole sky full of fireworks by the time he'd finished making love with her.

'I wanted to wear them for you today, Mac,' she murmured, bending close to his ear and nibbling on it while she ran her fingers through the silky thickness of his hair. 'Unfortunately, they don't quite fit me at the moment so I had to go shopping today to find some temporary replacements. You've no idea how difficult it was to find anything in scarlet to fit this sort of shape.'

While she'd been talking her free hand had been slipping the buttons of her maternity smock open.

Now she pushed the edges of the smock apart to reveal the pale swelling curves of her breasts cupped in the most decadent of lacy bras.

This was one area of her body that had really benefited from her pregnancy, and she was still surprised every time she glanced down and caught sight of her first really voluptuous cleavage.

Their two rings gleamed softly in the subdued light as they nestled in the swelling curve of her breasts, somehow enhancing their pale bounty.

'You probably wouldn't recognise them if you saw them, and they're so much more sensitive than they were,' she continued as she took both of his hands in hers and brought them up to cup her newly developed fullness.

'You used to say that they might be small, but they were just the right size to fit your hands. Now you've really got your hands full to overflowing.'

She moved his hands slightly against her so that the lace rasped softly over the skin of his palms.

'Can you feel that, Mac?' she asked softly. 'Can you feel the silkiness of the fabric and the pattern of the flowers woven into the lace? Can you feel the way my breasts fill the cups, and the way the warmth of my skin has transferred to the silk?'

She had to pause a moment while she caught her breath, amazed by how much she was becoming aroused. Already her nipples had grown hard, and if Mac weren't in a coma, he would have commented on it.

The fact that Mac would have commented on it was reason enough for her to speak about it. After all, she would only be reinforcing his natural traits from before the accident.

'Can you feel them, Mac? Can you feel the way my nipples are pushing against the fabric? Here…' With sudden inspiration she released one of his hands and pulled the scarlet fabric aside so that her pale flesh was cupped directly in his other hand.

She closed her eyes and groaned softly as the sensations poured through her in a flood.

'It's been so long since I've felt your hands touching me,' she moaned, her voice husky with arousal. 'In all these months I've been stroking you and exercising you, touching you all over as I've washed you and dried you and rubbed cream into your skin. I hadn't realised how much I'd missed being touched. Oh, Mac, I love you.'

She ran out of words to describe the maelstrom of emotions engendered by the simple contact between his hand and her breast and fell silent, sitting in the half-light for just a few precious seconds while she pretended that the last months had just been a bad dream.

She's here again. It's her voice and her touch and the smell of…of soap or perfume or skin…whatever it is that tells me she's here.

And how long has it been since I discovered I can tell her moods from her voice and her touch? Just one more reason why I need to know what the connection is between us…

Today she seems tense. Her hand and her voice are both shaking. Is she unhappy? Is something wrong?

If only I could ask… But all I can do is listen to her voice and try to concentrate so that the words make sense.

Sometimes she paints pictures in my mind with her

words, drawing them out of the mists and darkness until they almost seem real.

Like the firelight warming a darkened room, and candles and flowers and laughter.

Loving words and kisses and touches as clothing is shed. The soft sound of fabric and the silky touch, and the even silkier feel of warm, naked skin spilling into my hand.

'Happy birthday' someone is saying inside my head, and the words are echoing round and round until I can't tell if she is saying them or I am remembering them from the time before...before I was like this.

'I love you...' someone is murmuring. So happy... Happy birthday...beautiful, sexy...Kara!

'Mac?' Kara gasped in shock as his hand twitched against her naked breast and she froze in disbelief. Had she imagined that tiny movement?

'Mac, can you hear me? It's Kara. Did you hear what I was saying?' she demanded urgently, not knowing whether to look at his hand cupped around her breast or at his face.

There it was again, a little stronger this time, almost as if he was flexing his fingers to gauge the new shape and weight of her breast.

'Oh, my God,' she breathed, totally unable to think of anything but the fact that Mac had finally started moving. 'I must tell Mike.'

She drew in a shuddering breath, all at once desperate to tell someone what had happened and yet loath to break this tenuous contact with the man she loved.

Suddenly she focused on the fact that she was sitting in the dimness with a coma patient's hand wrapped around her naked breast, and a blush flared up her throat and into her face hot enough to light up the room.

Reluctantly she laid his hand back on the bed and fumbled to straighten her clothing, having to fight to force the buttons back through the holes with shaky fingers.

'I—I'll be back in a minute, Mac,' she stammered, almost tripping over her own feet in her hurry to get someone to page Mike. 'I promise I won't be long.'

She stumbled out into the corridor and made straight for the ward, sure somebody would be willing to contact Mike for her.

'I think he's probably at home by now. Either that or he's gone to the bonfire party,' Gaynor told her. 'He did a round of the patients before he went. Is there a problem with Mac? I could get the professor if you need him.'

Kara was torn between sharing her news with everyone who would stand still long enough and waiting until Mike had been to evaluate what had happened.

But that meant calling him at home and she had no idea where she'd put the piece of paper with Sue's new address and telephone number. Had she written it in her little book, was it somewhere in the bottom of her bag or had she lost it completely?

'Kara, is there a problem? I could try to contact him on his mobile number if it's urgent.'

'Please. Yes,' Kara said eagerly. 'Could you try his mobile number? I need to have a word with him.'

She was almost hopping from one foot to the other

while she waited for Gaynor to look the number up and then dial on an outside line.

'Mike? It's Kara,' she said when Gaynor handed her the phone. 'I'm sorry to disturb you, but could you possibly come to have a look at Mac? I was talking to him and he…and he… Oh, please, how long will it take you to get here?'

'Less than five minutes,' Mike said rather breathlessly. 'I'm on my mobile phone and if you look out of the window you'll probably see me taking a short cut across the grass to get to the main entrance.'

For a second Kara couldn't think why he would be going the long way round to get to the unit, but then she remembered that it was dark now and the number of accessible entrances were reduced at night to make security tighter.

'Hurry, Mike,' she pleaded, but the connection had already been cut so he was probably already inside the building.

'Thanks, Gaynor,' she said hurriedly, handing the dead phone back to her. 'I'll be waiting for Mike in Mac's room.'

'What's happening?' Gaynor called after her, obviously intrigued, but although she heard the question Kara didn't have time to stop and answer. After Mike had seen Mac would be soon enough.

By the time Mike arrived she was sitting at Mac's side again with his hand clasped in one of hers. Her other hand was wrapped tightly around their rings as she tried to concentrate long enough to remember some prayers.

The temptation was very great to demand that he squeeze her hand again, just to make certain that she hadn't imagined his response, but she was so afraid that she might cause a problem that she hardly dared to breathe.

'What's happened?' Mike demanded as soon as he entered the room. Sue followed him in and the way the two of them were wrapped up in warm clothing told her that they must have been at the firework display. She'd almost forgotten all about the noise and the flashes with everything that had happened since.

'I was talking to him about firework night and the fact that it's my birthday, and I was reminding him of what we did last year. You remember, Sue?' She turned to her friend. 'I told you about the meal he'd prepared and the candles and flowers.'

The more intimate details about the scarlet lingerie and the night of passion it had sparked had always remained secret between the two of them.

'I was holding his hand and…and suddenly he flexed his fingers. I asked him if he could hear what I was saying and he flexed them again. Then I phoned you.'

Mike performed some simple tests to check Mac's responses, and though Kara watched carefully she couldn't detect any signs that Mac was responding in any way differently to yesterday or the day before. The neutral expression on Mike's face wasn't much help either.

'Well?' she demanded eagerly.

'I want you to do exactly what you were doing before,' Mike said, stepping back to give her room.

'Exactly?' Kara glanced around the room. The main light had been switched on and there were several of the unit's nurses standing by the door, drawn by the unexpected air of excitement. She was going to die of embarrassment if she had to do that again in front of so many witnesses.

'Well, he hasn't responded to me so it might be something you were doing that triggered a response,' Mike explained logically.

Kara sat gingerly in the chair and took hold of Mac's hand again, knowing that whether the next few minutes were successful or not she wouldn't know where to put herself.

'Hello, Mac. It's Kara,' she said softly. 'I was just telling Mike about our conversation…about my last birthday. About the meal you served me in front of the fire with the flowers and the candles. And about the present you gave me all wrapped up in red paper with golden streamers.'

Nothing was happening and a sick dread was beginning to take hold of her. Had she wanted him to move so much that she'd actually fooled herself into believing that it had happened?

'Do you remember, Mac?' she murmured, and brought his hand up to press an individual kiss to each knuckle. She slid her fingers between his from the back of his hand so that his palm was spread wide and pressed a kiss to the centre of his palm.

She thought she'd imagined the movement at first but then his fingers curved inward until his fingertips stroked across one cheek. Had he mistaken the touch of her face in his hand for the press of her breast earlier?

'Mac?'

The single word was all she could manage with her heart in her throat. The waiting seemed endless but it probably wasn't longer that a couple of seconds before he slowly repeated the gesture. Kara closed her eyes and breathed a prayer of gratitude.

It might not be much, but it was so much more than everyone had expected and, as far as she was concerned, it was just another small step on his epic journey.

'His eyelids are flickering,' Mike pointed out softly, and her own eyes flew open to look. 'And the monitors are all picking up extra activity—pulse, respiration...'

'More connections,' she murmured, fighting the hot press of tears as she stared down into Mac's beloved face. 'Oh, Mac, you should be glad you're not a horse or I'd have sent you to the glue factory long ago.'

'As it is, you're going to continue to take his recovery slowly and steadily,' Mike finished for her on a more upbeat note.

'And when he's fully recovered, *then* you'll think about shooting him,' Sue added cheekily.

'Is this a really good sign?' Kara begged when the rest of the staff had dispersed, once again leaving the four of them in the room.

'Yes, it's a really good sign that there is a lot going on inside his brain but, no, it doesn't mean that in five minutes' time he's going to sit up and hold a conversation with you, before inviting you out to a disco.'

'So what you're saying is that, in a way, this movement doesn't change anything. I've still got to do the same things for him and to him while we wait for the damaged side of his brain to recover or develop new pathways.'

'You've got it,' Mike said with a grimace. 'Kara,

if there was some way this process could be speeded up, you know I would do it.'

'But you don't want to risk burning out any more of the old connections or scrambling any of the new ones,' Kara finished for him. 'It's all right, Mike. I understand. But you won't mind if I have a little celebration of my own over the fact that he moved for the first time in…' Her brain was still too scrambled to do the maths.

'You'll probably start to notice all sorts of movements now that his brain has decided it's ready to allow the first one.'

'Should I ask him to move?'

'You probably won't need to. He'll respond better to what you're saying and doing—for example, when you're doing his mobilisation you might suddenly find that he starts taking some of the weight of his limb.'

'The sooner the better,' Kara joked with a gesture towards her non-existent waistline. 'I'm already carrying more weight than I want to.'

She tried to apologise for disturbing their evening but Mike and Sue wouldn't hear of it.

'He's not just my patient, he's also my friend,' Mike reminded her. 'Any time you want me to come, you only have to ask.'

Even after the two of them had gone, the atmosphere in the room seemed different.

Somehow, the fact that Mac had responded to her made it seem as if he'd become closer, as if an impenetrable barrier which had stood between them ever since the accident had lifted just a little bit to allow a brief, rudimentary communication.

'We're getting there, Mac,' she whispered fiercely.

'It's taking a long time, but we're getting there, and when you're well again it will have been worth every minute.'

Kara is here...my Kara is here...and now that I know who she is, suddenly I know how important it is to fight the darkness that tries to claim me.

It is still hard...desperately hard...to sort the thoughts and ideas out inside my head. It's as if there's a huge hole where everything disappears...

But Kara is here and she won't let me disappear into the darkness of the hole... Kara will hold my hand and help me find a way out into the light...

Over the following month Kara sometimes felt as if she was just holding her breath, waiting for something to happen.

After the excitement of Mac's first physical response she hadn't honestly believed that it would take too much longer.

Oh, she knew she'd reassured Mike that she wasn't expecting instant miracles, but it wasn't true. There had been so many months when the only progress she had been able to chart had been the fact that Mac hadn't got any worse.

Now that she'd had concrete proof of the rehabilitation work that had been going on all along inside his head, she'd had absolute faith that it would just be a matter of days before he opened his eyes and spoke to her.

It hadn't happened, and here it was the end of November, with her maternity leave looming large on the horizon.

Apart from anything else, she was frustrated by not

knowing when Mac was going to make his next stride forward. Until she knew how fast and how well he was going to recover, she didn't know what sort of place to look for, ready for when she had to move out of the staff accommodation.

Was she just going to need something small enough for herself and the new baby, or was she going to need something big enough for Mac, too?

Then there were the other considerations. Was he going to need a ground-floor flat with wheelchair access, or a flat with a lift, or would his recovery permit him to tackle stairs?

At no stage did she allow herself to even contemplate the fact that he wasn't going to recover so that they could be together at last.

Obviously, there were going to be huge gaps in his memory and his knowledge of things that had happened while he was unconscious.

In spite of the number of times she must have mentioned her pregnancy, he probably wouldn't know anything about the baby until he opened his eyes and saw that she was pregnant. And there were other things around him that had changed.

Mike worked at St Augustine's now, and was married to Sue—both events that had happened since Mac's accident. There was also the worldwide fuss about the fact that in just a matter of weeks the twentieth century would become the twenty-first.

She knew of members of St Augustine's staff who had been prepared to pay silly amounts of money so that they wouldn't be stuck on duty when the clock struck midnight.

It was a shame she would be about a fortnight away

from giving birth or she would gladly have added to her savings if someone else were willing to bribe her.

As it was, Sue and Mike had invited her to join them to mark the occasion, but she'd decided that she was going to see the new century in with Mac.

When he'd been struck down, the only concern she'd had about the new millennium had been whether the bugs would all have been exterminated from the hospital's computer system and all the computerised equipment. She hadn't realised exactly how many items of equipment, large and small, there were scattered throughout every department which relied on tiny date-coded chips.

She just hoped that the whizkid computer buffs who had been working their way through room by room had covered everything by the time the clock reached the fateful hour. The thought of patients such as Mac had been, dependent on a computer-controlled ventilator for every breath and suddenly connected to machinery that refused to work, was a nightmare.

Multiply that by the number of beds and the number of departments and the number of hospitals… It sounded like a catastrophe, waiting to happen.

'You stay where you are until everything's all been sorted out,' she advised, smoothing her hand over the pronounced bulge of the baby which would soon need a circus tent to cover it.

She was rewarded with a fierce kick just as she pushed open the door to the neurology unit.

'Hey, that wasn't very nice,' she murmured as she circled her fingertips over the pointy little protrusion. What was it—an elbow, a knee, a heel? Perhaps even a fist?

'It's a good job I know you or I'd wonder about this tendency of yours to talk to yourself,' Alison teased.

'If I'm not talking to Mac, I'm talking to the baby,' Kara admitted. 'I'm just looking forward to having someone reply.'

'It must seem as if you've been pregnant for ever.'

'At least two years,' Kara agreed. 'When he or she arrives there's a small list of things I'm really looking forward to doing—like cutting my toenails without needing arms six feet long and a full-length mirror, and eating without having someone try to kick everything back up the way it came, and being able to roll over in bed without needing a crane.'

'What about a bath? You know, a really good wallow,' Alison suggested.

'I've got the wallowing off pat, without needing a bath,' Kara joked. 'But you're right. At the moment, the bath in the staff accommodation is too narrow for me to be able to get out as easily as I get in.'

'And you don't particularly want to be rescued when you're in that condition.'

They were both chuckling at the idea of firemen breaking down a bathroom door to rescue a female looking like a beached whale stranded in a bath when their paths divided.

'Hello, Mac, my love,' she said and bent awkwardly to kiss him. 'How have you been today?'

She settled herself in the chair beside him and reached for his hand, the way she had ever since the first time she'd seen him lying so still and silent.

'Only a few more days before I stop being Obstetrics and Gynaecology staff and wait to become a patient.'

The sharp, pointy object gave her another jab and she shifted a little to try to allow both of them a little more room for comfort. It would have been easier if she let go of Mac's hand, but that wasn't negotiable. The fact that Mac responded to contact with her was the best reason she knew for reinforcing that contact at every opportunity.

'At least the ward's quieter these days,' she said, filling him in on her day at work. 'We always have a lot of babies born around September—after all, that's when any "accidents" that happen as a result of Christmas and New Year parties are due.'

It wasn't a problem she'd ever had to worry about. Not being the party sort, she'd never been tempted to take risks under the influence of alcohol or in any other way. Then she'd met Mac and the attraction between them had been so strong that a lifetime's principles had flown out of the window. Within weeks she had willingly moved in with him, knowing that she had met the man with whom she was going to spend the rest of her life.

'There are a number of babies due over the Christmas and New Year period, and a few booked in at the same time as I'm due, but, of course, that can change day by day as some arrive early and others go beyond their due dates.'

She did hope hers—*theirs*—was going to arrive on time. She'd seen how depressed some of the mums became when they'd got themselves all prepared for a particular date…and then nothing happened.

'Still, when the apple's ripe, he'll fall,' she quoted. 'I've even heard of one couple who went cross-country on a motorbike to try to shake the baby into moving! Of course, nothing happened.'

Another vicious onslaught with the pointy protrusion caught her by surprise, and Kara had to draw in a deep breath and release it slowly while she tried to soothe the over-active baby with rhythmic stroking.

After several long minutes it seemed to work and her hand grew still.

With the absence of the sound of her hand on the fabric of her top she suddenly became aware of another rhythmic sound in the room.

A quick glance confirmed that she and Mac were still alone, but a glance at the omnipresent monitors had her leaping to her feet.

'You're too warm, Mac. What's the matter?' she demanded, her hand confirming what her eyes had spotted. His forehead was coated with a fine film of sweat and there was an increasing wheeze to his breathing.

CHAPTER NINE

'PNEUMONIA?' Kara gasped and grabbed onto the side rail of the bed to stop her knees from collapsing. 'He *can't* have pneumonia!'

Mike straightened up from his examination, his forehead pleated with worry.

'I'm sending blood, urine and sputum samples to the lab before we start Mac on any drugs, and I'll need a chest X-ray before we can be absolutely certain, but you know as well as I do that it's one of the most common infections caught in hospital.'

'But how did Mac get it, and why now—after all this time with no problems at all?'

'Although it seems as if he's just been lying there for months on end, his whole system has been under massive stress ever since the accident. Knowing how many bugs there are knocking about in a hospital, it's almost miraculous that he *hasn't* had anything like this before. The fact that he's both bedridden and unconscious are two large strikes against him.'

'But what are you going to do now? If it's staphylococcal pneumonia you can't afford to wait for results...' She couldn't bear to finish the thought. *Staphylococcus aureus* had become resistant to so many drugs now that it had a death rate of between fifteen and forty per cent, and that was with patients already in hospital and within reach of constant medical assistance.

'Because of Mac's situation, I'll start him on a

third-generation cephalosporin, but if he doesn't start responding fairly quickly I'll put him straight on vancomycin.'

Kara blinked. She knew vancomycin was used as a last line of defence against MRSA when every other avenue had been tried. Did Mike's willingness to prescribe it so soon signal the fact that Mac was more seriously ill than she'd realised, or was it a measure of his personal involvement in the case?

It felt very strange to have to stand back while other people set up drips and withdrew specimens and samples. It had been a long time since Mac had needed to rely on oxygen but in just that short space of time he was beginning to struggle for breath. Kara tightened her grip on the two rings hidden under her smock and breathed a sigh of relief when she saw the mask go on over his face.

'Don't forget, everyone,' Mike called over the mixture of noises in the crowded room. 'In case this *is* a case of MRSA, I want rigorous barrier nursing. This must *not* spread to any of the patients in the main unit.'

Kara knew what was going to happen now. Everyone who came into Mac's room would have to wear protective clothing that would be discarded as they left. Nothing that came into the room, or that came into contact with Mac himself, would be allowed to carry whatever infection he was fighting out of the room.

Gradually, the room emptied until Mike was left standing in front of Kara.

'You need to go, too,' he said quietly. 'You can't afford to risk infecting your mums and babies with something like this.'

'But…that would mean I couldn't visit Mac,' she exclaimed. 'I can't just leave him to go through this alone. He's depending on me to be here for him.'

'So are your patients,' he pointed out. 'Would you be able to live with yourself if you infected one of them with MRSA and they died?'

Mike knew she would never be able to do that.

'I'll apply for compassionate leave,' she said on a sudden inspiration. 'Or I could apply to start my maternity leave a little early. It's only days before I was due to leave anyway.'

'But, Kara—'

'Please, Mike. You know how long I've been waiting and working for Mac to recover. I can't just abandon him now when he's ill. He wouldn't understand.'

'And what about the baby? How can you reconcile the fact that you'll be putting him or her at risk?'

'I've been in contact with Mac at least twice a day and I've already held his hand and kissed him since I came into the room today. That was before I noticed there was a problem with his breathing, so if I've caught it, it's already too late to send me away. But, in case I haven't already caught it, I'll comply with the barrier nursing restrictions, too.'

She knew she sounded as if she was begging, and knew, too, that her heart must be in her eyes as she looked up at his stern expression.

'Please, Mike,' she whispered, with a quick glance across at Mac. 'If it's MRSA there's up to a forty per cent mortality rate. If Mac's going to die, I've got to be here with him. I've *got* to.'

Can't breathe… Lungs full of treacle and heavy…so heavy…

It's so hard to drag air in...and so tired of fighting...so tired...

But Kara is there...still talking to me...still saying I love you...

It would be so easy to stop fighting...but that would mean leaving Kara...never hearing her voice or feeling her touch...never opening my eyes to see her there beside me...

I can't leave her...not now that I know who she is...not now that I know I love her, too...but I can't breathe...

'He's going down!' somebody exclaimed just before the monitors went mad. 'Respiratory arrest!' Her hand slapped on the emergency button and the alarm began to sound. There was no need to make a separate call for the crash team because the system was all interlinked.

Kara had been sitting beside Mac for nearly an hour and had been able to see that he was struggling for breath even with the oxygen to help.

She'd never thought that he would simply stop breathing. *That* was a scene out of her worst nightmare.

'What happened?' Mike demanded, still thrusting his hands into the arms of a disposable gown as he entered the room at a run, the crash cart following close behind.

Kara wanted to wrap Mac in her arms and scream at them to hurry, for God's sake, hurry, but she still had enough sense to know that the best thing she could do was get out of the way.

'Dammit, Mac, don't you *dare* do this!' Mike swore when he saw what was going on.

His disposable gloves had barely snapped in position when he was reaching out for the resuscitation tray.

From her post in the furthest corner of the room Kara could clearly see the crash team swarming into action, her eyes feverishly following their every move as they grabbed the equipment from their trolley.

It took Mike mere seconds to have Mac intubated and he immediately began ventilating him in rhythm while one of the nurses performed cardiac massage.

Both of them reluctantly gave up their posts to members of the crash team, but that didn't mean that Mike was prepared to stand back and wait idly by while others cared for his friend. Immediately he was on the phone, checking the results of the latest tests.

'Please, Mac, please,' Kara whispered, both hands wrapped around their precious rings as her heart tried to beat its way out of her chest. 'Please, don't leave me.'

Her heart nearly stopped when everybody suddenly straightened away from Mac's body, and for one dreadful moment she thought they were giving up.

'Hands off. Shocking,' a male voice said, and Kara saw Mac's body arch up off the bed with the jolt of the electric current.

'Still fibrillating. Try again,' said another faceless voice.

'Hands off. Shocking again,' the first voice said, and once more Mac's body jerked viciously.

There was an unearthly silence for a second before the monitors detected a steady beat.

'Normal sinus rhythm,' the voice reported with a tinge of deliverance.

It was a good job Kara had propped herself in a

corner because she was certain that was the only thing that kept her upright as relief flooded through her.

'That was the last thing he needed,' Mike said in disgust. 'How long was he down?'

'Less than a minute before chest compressions started, and then you intubated him,' Kara heard the young woman reply.

'Probably not long enough to do him any damage…if he hadn't already been fighting the effects of a head injury,' Mike said, clearly worried. 'As for the effects of the electrical discharge…'

'We've got another problem now,' reported the same voice, his tone sharp enough to cut through all the other conversations. 'His chest isn't moving properly on one side. I think he's got tension pneumothorax.'

Kara's eyes flew to Mac again and she realised that even from the other side of the room she could see the blue-tinged evidence of cyanosis. The monitors, too, were sounding out their warning of Mac's rapid, weak pulse.

'Chest decompression, fast, or we're going to lose him,' Mike snapped.

Kara was sure they must be working as quickly as they could but it seemed to her as if everything was happening in slow motion.

It was a procedure she'd seen many times since she started her nursing training but it was one that never failed to make her hold her breath.

Every second counted as Mac's chest rapidly began to fill up with the air escaping from a puncture wound in one lung. Each breath allowed more air to escape and the accumulated air was gradually exerting more and more pressure on both lungs. With the pressure putting kinks in the vessels returning blood to the right side of the heart, his newly restored cardiac function was under threat again.

An antibacterial swab was wiped over the second intercostal space and then a large bore through-the-needle catheter was inserted along the upper border of the rib.

Kara was watching so closely that she actually saw the needle 'pop' into the pleural space.

Immediately, the pressurised air began to vent out through the catheter even as the needle was withdrawn and the catheter was taped in position.

For a moment everyone stood still, waiting and listening as the pulse rate dropped towards a more normal rhythm.

'Anything else you want to throw at us to see if we know our stuff?' quipped one of the crash team, and everyone chuckled wryly as they began to gather up their discarded supplies.

'Now for the bad news,' Mike said and they all paused. 'We're waiting for confirmation, but we think he's got MRSA.'

'Bloody barrier nursing,' the joker muttered in disgust.

'Sorry. No time to warn you on the way in,' Mike said. 'There's a trolley full of clean supplies just outside the door.'

'Come on, then, Caroline, get your kit off!' the joker teased one of the other members of the team. 'I've been dying to say that to you for ages.'

Out of the corner of her eye Kara saw the forbearance on the beautiful nurse's face and guessed that she'd been putting up with comments like that for a long time.

'Mike?' she called softly, still waiting in her corner until she'd been given permission to approach Mac again.

'Oh, Lord, Kara, I completely forgot you were still standing there. Come and take the weight off your feet.' He gestured towards a chair and Kara pulled it across until it was once more in her usual place beside Mac's bed.

Mike had returned immediately to his conversation with the senior member of the crash team and all she could do was wait until he was free to tell her what Mac's prognosis was.

She'd heard him worrying out loud about the effects of the shocks they'd had to use to get Mac's heart working. What she needed to know was how far back it would have put Mac's progress.

'One month to go,' Kara announced as she settled down beside Mac after attending her latest antenatal examination.

Now that she was on maternity leave she was able to spend twice as much time with him as before.

'And it's less than two weeks to Christmas now.'

It was also just over two weeks since she'd nearly lost Mac to a bout of MRSA, complicated by a tension pneumothorax.

It would be a long time before the images of Mac fighting for his life would fade from her mind's eye. He'd been lucky not to develop any of the abscesses so common with *staphylococcus aureus* infections, but it had still taken him a long time to come off the ventilator again.

The one problem Mike had been most worried about seemed to have passed Mac by. In spite of the desperate measures they'd had to use to get his heart beating again, Mac had apparently suffered no setback in his neurological progress.

'You seem to be responding more every day,' Kara said aloud. She found it amusing that it seemed to be a case of like father, like child. Neither of them seemed to stay completely still for more than a few minutes at a time.

Mac's file now resembled several volumes of an encyclopaedia, one of them chronicling Kara's observations.

After the respiratory collapse Mike had reassessed Mac's condition and was able to tell Kara that he was now scoring a good nine on the Glasgow coma scale, and as anything over an eight was taken to indicate a good chance of recovery she'd been ecstatic.

These days she often saw Mac going through periods of REM sleep, the rapid eye movements suggesting that he had started to dream again, and he was even responding readily to clear, simple orders.

'That certainly makes your exercises a lot easier for me,' she commented, grateful for anything that lightened the load on her complaining back. That hadn't been helped by her recent change of abode, even though Sue and Mike had insisted on doing all the lifting.

'It's only a few minutes' walk away from the hospital,' she told him, certain, in spite of what Mike said, that he was not only taking everything in but also understanding it. 'Mike and Sue found the house because they were looking for something more convenient for themselves. The landlord at their old place didn't want to have to do all those repairs after the water tank sprang a leak in the roof so they weren't going to stay there.'

It was an end-of-terrace Victorian house which had recently been divided into two flats, and both of them were empty.

She'd been a little worried when Sue had told her that Mike was buying the whole house and was offering to be her landlord if she wanted to move into the ground-floor flat. It was only when she'd insisted that she would pay a fair market rent for the accommodation that they'd all agreed.

She wouldn't allow herself to dwell on the fact that it was going to be absolutely perfect for Mac to move to when he finally emerged from the coma.

'Oh, Mac, I hope it happens soon,' she whispered as she threaded her fingers through his and held on tightly. 'I do so want you to be with me. There are so many things happening around you and Mike says that you won't remember anything of what I'm telling you, but…I do want you here to share them with me.'

At the moment they were surrounded by the run-up to the annual chaos of Christmas in a large hospital, with more and more decorations springing up every time she turned a corner.

In her own department there had already been the start of the usual rash of children given seasonal names. Nicholas, Holly and Noel were bound to appear, but this year there had also been an Angela and a Donna just to add a bit of variety.

'Sue has been keeping me up to date on some of our patients,' she told Mac. 'Most of them are progressing perfectly normally, but there have been two very upsetting discoveries just this week.'

One was a lady she'd met on her last shift in the

antenatal clinic. 'It was her first visit because she was working full time. She'd waited until about four months after her last period before she came, and today Sue was able to fit her into a gap in the ultrasound schedule.'

Kara had spoken to Sue about the lady. Something about her condition was definitely wrong and after poor Mrs Lidyatt's stillbirth she didn't want to take any chances.

'It was a dreadful shock when the poor woman had to be told she had an enormous ovarian cyst. She wasn't pregnant at all.' Still, even if the surgeon decided he had to remove the whole ovary, the chances were that she would be able to conceive normally from the other one.

'The worst one Sue saw was a lady who looked nearly full term and had just come along to find out where we were for when she went into labour.'

The poor woman hadn't been as lucky as the lady with the ovarian cyst. The surgeon had brought her in as an emergency case because he thought he was dealing with a particularly urgent case of fibroids. It was only when he sent a section up to the lab that the diagnosis of cancer was made.

It had been too late to catch it—metastases were already spreading rapidly throughout her body, and by the time she recovered enough from the surgery to leave the hospital she would probably need to move into a hospice.

Sue's tales of horror had made Kara very glad that she'd been given a clean bill of health at each of her antenatal appointments. Since the initial days after Mac's accident she'd been very careful to take very good care of this child they'd created between them.

Now all she needed was for Mac to wake up to share the event with her.

Even in a ward where patients were so seriously ill, Christmas had crept in.

Visitors to the neurology department had brought in cards and tinsel to decorate the heads of the beds and there were bunches of balloons and sprigs of mistletoe appearing in unexpected places.

Someone had tied a piece of mistletoe to the head of Mac's bed and the attached note told the two of them that they now had a good excuse for kissing.

'As if we needed an excuse,' Kara said when Sue laughed. She squeezed Mac's hand and when he squeezed back she jumped, still not accustomed to the fact that he'd begun to reciprocate.

Kara felt the soppy grin creep over her face when she remembered the first time his lips had moved under hers when she'd kissed him. She'd been so excited about it that the next time she bent towards him she'd been as nervous as a teenager on her first date.

The first time Mac had opened his eyes had taken her by surprise, too. True, it had only been as a result of pain when she'd been stretching out his hamstrings, but now he would sometimes open them when she was talking to him.

She had to remember not to allow her dismay to show when she couldn't find the wicked spark in his familiar dark brown eyes. It would come, she promised herself. One day, *her* Mac would be back…she only wished it could be in time for Christmas. That would be the best present in the world.

'Happy Christmas, Sue,' Kara said when her friend opened the door. 'I wanted to give you these before

I went into the hospital.'

She handed over two brightly wrapped parcels and stepped back, the carrier bag over her other arm bumping against her ungainly body.

'Are you sure you don't want to join us?' Mike asked as he came to join Sue at the door. 'You'd be more than welcome.'

'Thank you very much for the invitation but I promised Mac I'd spend the day with him. Anyway, this is your first Christmas together. You don't want me in the way if you decide you want to put dinner off for other pursuits.'

Sue chuckled and turned pink but Mike tried to brazen it out. 'What *is* she talking about, dear?' he demanded with an air of innocence.

'If he doesn't know by now, you're doing something wrong, Sue,' Kara teased her friend, and waved them goodbye.

'Happy Christmas, Mac,' Kara murmured as she bent forward awkwardly to kiss him.

Now that she was so huge, the safety railings definitely made life difficult for her, but that didn't mean she was going to forgo her kiss.

'I've brought you some presents,' she announced as she began to slide the first one out of the carrier bag.

The crackling sound must have caught Mac's attention because he turned his head towards the sound.

'Ah, you heard that, did you?' she said with a chuckle. 'You always did like unwrapping surprises...as well as giving them.' She had a brief flash of a certain set of scarlet underwear but forced herself to switch the memory off. There was no way she could indulge in any re-enactment scenes in the middle of Christmas Day when anyone could walk in…even Father Christmas.

'That *would* give him something to ho-ho-ho about,' she murmured with a private grin. 'Now, do you want to help me unwrap your presents?'

She placed the first one on the bed beside him and placed his hand on top of it. Hooking his fingers carefully under the edge of the wrapping paper, she began to tear.

The familiar sound prompted Mac to open his eyes again briefly, then open them wider when the bright gleam of metallic golden baubles on a dark green background caught his attention.

'Keep tearing,' Kara instructed. 'I know you'd rather do that than open it slowly and carefully. Shall we use two hands?'

According to Mike, the fact that Mac had been almost completely ambidextrous before the accident had probably played a significant part in his brain's response to the stimulation she'd been giving him. And she'd always teased him that the only use he put it to was ripping his presents open twice as fast as anyone else.

'It's not terribly exciting,' she apologised. 'It's only a dressing-gown, but it is a pure silk brocade and lined with silk.' She stroked his hand over the sensuous fabric, letting him feel the contrast between the golden figures of coiled dragons and the sleek black satin.

'It will feel gorgeous against your skin,' she promised. 'Very opulent, perhaps even decadent.'

She took hold of a handful of fabric and smoothed

it against his cheek then over his shoulders and down his chest. 'Doesn't that feel wonderful?' she asked, and nearly jumped out of her skin when he groaned in apparent agreement.

'Do you like that, Mac? Do you want me to do it again?' She watched his eyelids flutter closed as she brought the heavy fabric up to his face again, this time lingering long enough to stroke it over both cheeks and over his forehead.

'It feels warm and cool at the same time, doesn't it?' she commented, as she watched a rash of goose-bumps spread from one side of his chest to the other. 'Can you feel it through the hairs on your arms?'

Once again the gliding touch was followed by goose-bumps, and it took her several seconds to realise what she was seeing.

'They're even, Mac,' she said excitedly. 'Your goose-bumps are even on both sides now. Wait till I tell Mike.'

Soft and smooth... She's stroking me with something soft and smooth and it's giving me the shivers.

Ah, but it's her voice that makes it perfect...a little husky so it seems to stroke my skin too.

Is her skin as soft as the thing she's using on my skin...? Softer, I would think, and instead of making me shiver it would make me burn.

Oh, the frustration of listening to her. I think I've even caught glimpses of her...either her or a dark-haired angel sitting beside me, but it's difficult to focus properly...

I don't understand why there's still this great void between me and the things going on out there. I can feel her touching me but it seems to be happening at

*a great distance. It's as if I'm surrounded by a cocoon
that prevents anything reaching me inside.*

*Time doesn't matter where I am because I can do
nothing to change my little world. If only she had the
power to tear down the cocoon—to force me to join
the world where she lives.*

'Just a few more hours and we'll be saying hello to
the new millennium,' Kara announced, as she tried to
make herself comfortable in her usual seat.

All day she'd been twitchy, unable to settle anywhere for long. She'd just been marching round
Mac's room for no good reason until she'd forced
herself to sit down again.

'Phew, I'll be glad when the next two weeks are
over,' she muttered. 'I feel as if I'm the same size as
a hippopotamus and with all the grace of a Centurion
tank. And I used to wonder what all the pregnant
mums were moaning for when they were so close to
the end. How are the mighty fallen!'

Her back had begun aching several hours previously, but it wasn't until she felt the slow, rolling
wave of muscles tightening that she suddenly realised
why she'd been feeling so uncomfortable.

'I don't know whether to hope that's just a
Braxton-Hicks contraction or whether to cross my fingers that it's the start of the real thing,' she said with
a nervous giggle. 'It's unlikely because the head
hasn't even engaged properly yet. Still, if they start
coming regularly, we might end up having one of the
first babies born in the new millennium.'

She noted the time and tried to settle down to one
of her usual rambling conversations with a man who
didn't reply, but while she was waiting to see if an-

other contraction was coming she couldn't really concentrate.

It took nearly twenty minutes for the second one to arrive and another fifteen for the third, before they settled at a steady ten minutes for several hours.

Once she was certain that it wasn't a false alarm, she phoned down to Sister Harris to warn her that she might have another candidate for motherhood arriving in the small hours of the morning. After that there was nothing to do but wait.

Outside the hospital she could hear the occasional firework being released ahead of time, and there were shouts and the hooting car horns every now and again as the excitement of the approaching milestone took hold.

At intervals she got up and wandered backwards and forwards, and she was suddenly unaccountably angry with Mac that he couldn't share this special time with her.

'Damn you, Mac,' she said through gritted teeth as yet another contraction dug its claws into her. She braced herself on the safety railing at the side of his bed and tightened her hands until the knuckles gleamed whitely through her skin.

'This is your baby as well as mine. The least you could do is— Ah-h!' She gave a little shriek as the baby almost seemed to turn itself inside out and in the process suddenly settled its head deep in the cradle of her pelvis.

CHAPTER TEN

SUDDENLY calm, Kara straightened up and moved as close as she could to Mac.

'I'm sorry I was so ratty,' she apologised as she took his hands in hers and kissed each of them. 'I know you aren't doing this on purpose but I just let my frustration get the better of me for a moment.'

She lowered herself to perch on the edge of her chair, concerned that she might not be able to get up again if she let herself get too comfortable.

When she had three contractions in the next fifteen minutes she realised that there was no chance of getting too comfortable. It was rapidly looking as if she wasn't even going to get the chance to see the New Year in with Mac.

Suddenly it seemed very important that she tried to make him understand what was happening.

She'd mentioned her pregnancy and the baby on many occasions over the long months since he'd had his accident, but this was here and now and the baby was going to be arriving shortly.

'Mac, I need to tell you something important,' she began, standing up to grasp his hands again to focus his attention. 'You need to listen carefully.'

She had to pause for a moment when just the act of standing up appeared to trigger another contraction. Was she going to have time to finally make him understand about their baby?

'Mac, we're having a baby,' she said slowly and

172

clearly. 'I was going to tell you about it when we went away together after the wedding, but then you had your accident.'

How could she condense the time between their wedding-day-that-never-was and tonight into something he could really understand? So many recovered coma patients had absolutely no memory of anything that had happened while they'd been unconscious, even though they'd seemed to be responding at the time. Would Mac remember what she was trying to tell him when he finally woke?

'All these months while you've been healing—while the damaged receptors and transmitters in your brain have been forming new routes so they can work again—the baby's been growing, and tonight he or she is going to be born.'

She saw a slight frown drawing his dark brows together in apparent response. Was he taking her words in or was she completely wasting her time?

The familiar ache started growing again, telling her that another contraction was on its way, and she had a sudden idea.

'Here, Mac. Feel,' she said abruptly, pulling her smock up with one hand and placing his palm over the increasing hardness of her belly.

It took a bit of manoeuvring, especially as the full force of the pain gripped her, but she managed to part her clothes so that his hand rested on her naked skin.

'Give me your other hand,' she directed, and was startled when he did it almost instantly, as if he had been waiting for her to ask. 'Now, can you feel this?'

She was panting with the effort of concentrating on so many things at once—the progress of the contraction, placing his hands on the evidence of their child *and* talking to him about what he was feeling.

'This is our baby,' she said more clearly when the contraction began to fade. She moved both of his hands around so that he could feel the way her skin was stretched over the large mound. While she was between contractions the rock-hard muscles had softened and she was able to cup his hand around some of the pointed bits that had been poking her so insistently for the last few months. She felt his hands stiffen in shock when one of them moved at his touch.

'This is our baby,' she repeated softly as she stroked his hands over and around the protrusion. 'This is the baby we made with our love.'

She had to stop speaking for a moment as another contraction hit her hard and fast. Her knees didn't want to hold her any more, and she was forced to grab for the safety rails.

Instead of Mac's hands falling away from her as soon as she let go of them, they stayed pressed against her as her belly grew as hard as a cannonball with the force of the contraction.

One part of her mind was relishing the unexpected connection between them, but Kara couldn't help realising that she was rapidly running out of time.

'Oh, God,' she groaned when she didn't think she was going to be able to summon up the energy to press the bell for help.

The sound of her voice seemed to startle Mac and his hands tightened briefly over her belly before, suddenly, he started stroking her.

It was just a jerky movement at first, as if the machinery controlling the movement was rusty from disuse, but by the time the contraction was fading he seemed to have learned how to make the movement soothing.

She would have loved to stay there and see what would happen next but she had finally run out of time.

'I love you, Mac,' she said as she reached out and pressed the call bell. 'I love you but I'll have to go now.'

She watched his eyebrows draw into a frown again but he still hadn't removed his hands from their tenuous contact with their child. Touched that he seemed to be making such an effort to understand, she placed her hands over his again and leaned forward just far enough to kiss him.

'I'll be back soon,' she promised with a quick glance at the clock. 'It might not be until the next century, but *we'll* be back soon.'

'It's a girl,' Margaret Harris declared with delight just twenty minutes later. 'She might be two weeks early but otherwise she's absolutely perfect. Perfect Apgar, too.'

Kara chuckled weakly. Trust Sister Harris to remember the important things.

Then she wasn't chuckling any more as her little daughter was placed in her arms.

With two dark-haired parents it was no surprise that her silky cap of hair was also dark, but at the moment her wide-open eyes were neither blue-grey like her own nor dark brown like her father's but the very deep blue of the newborn. While Kara did the time-honoured thing and counted her daughter's perfect little fingers and toes she wondered how long it would take before she would know what colour her eyes would end up.

Before she could ask Sister Harris she suddenly became aware that for several minutes there had been a great deal of noise going on somewhere outside the room.

'What on earth is all that?' she asked in amazement. Apart from the occasional groan from a woman in labour and the sound of babies crying, the department was usually very peaceful.

'That's the dawn of the new millennium, I believe,' Margaret Harris said. 'You were too busy to notice, but just as little madam there was emerging into the world, every bell and whistle and siren in the town went off, the sky was filled with fireworks and everyone started shouting, "Happy New Millennium,"—including any patients who were still awake!'

She'd barely finished speaking when the telephone added its strident summons to the cacophony.

'Sister Harris,' she said crisply, then listened for a moment. 'Yes, she's here, and mother and baby are both doing well.'

She was silent for a moment before she suddenly held the phone out to Kara with a broad smile. 'It's for you,' she said, and just before she turned away Kara was almost certain that she saw a glint of tears in her superior's eyes.

'Hello?' she said, half-afraid of what she would hear. Who on earth would be calling her here? 'Mike! Why are you calling? You should be celebrating with Sue.'

'Oh, I was, believe me,' Mike said, the crackle accompanying his voice telling her that he was using his mobile phone again. 'Then I had a phone call and now Sue and I are on our way into the hospital.'

'Oh, Mike, you didn't have to come in tonight to

see the baby. It's a lovely idea but tomorrow would have been soon enough.'

'Actually, Kara, until I spoke to Sister Harris just now I didn't know the baby had been born. I was ringing to tell you that Alison just phoned me from Mac's room and told me where to find you. It seems that Mac woke up just as the bells started ringing and he's asking to see you.'

Margaret Harris must have guessed how stunned Kara would be because she was there, ready to take the baby from her, when shock suddenly robbed Kara's muscles of any strength.

'Mac?' she squeaked, certain that she must have misheard. She must still be light-headed on the gas and air mixture she'd been breathing. 'Mac's awake? And he wants to see me?'

Kara wanted to hurry to Mac's room immediately but there was the little matter of delivering the after-birth to attend to first.

It was nearly an hour before Sister Harris finally gave her permission to climb gingerly into a wheel-chair for the journey back to Mac's room.

'Mike!' she exclaimed when she saw him waiting for her by the bank of lifts, his face wreathed in a broad smile.

With a few words Mike dismissed the porter and took charge of the wheelchair handles himself.

'How are mother and baby doing?' he asked with another smile for the two of them. 'It's all wrapped up in white so I've no idea what variety it is.'

'She's so beautiful that it's obvious she's a girl,' Kara said instantly, then groaned because even with her new baby daughter in her arms there was only one thing she wanted to know. 'Oh, Mike, tell me. How is Mac? What happened to bring him out of it?'

'You'll have to ask him yourself,' Mike said as he expertly reversed through a pair of swing doors to open them with his back. 'All he'll say to anyone else is that he wants to see you.'

'And he really is all right?' she demanded. 'I mean, *really…?*'

'He's very weak and it's going to take an enormous amount of patience and determination to get him going again, but with you in his corner I wouldn't be surprised if he confounds the experts yet again.'

Mike's words bolstered Kara but they also served as a warning to her not to expect too much when she first saw Mac. After the massive damage he'd received and after all these months, he would probably be a completely different person—one she would have to get to know all over again.

Then the door of his room opened and as soon as she saw his eyes she knew that *her* Mac was back.

'Kara,' he said as soon as he saw her, his voice a husky croak she nearly didn't recognise. 'Kara,' he repeated, and held one shaky hand out towards her.

'Oh, Mac,' she breathed as Mike pushed her forward in answer to the summons, tears of joy beginning to overflow. 'Oh, Mac, you've come back. How? After all this time. Why now?'

The wheelchair was lower than the chair she usually sat on beside his bed, but this time Mac could turn to look at her.

'That. That's why,' he said laboriously, as if he had to search for each syllable, and he pointed at the white-swaddled bundle cradled in her arms. 'Your baby. My baby.' He spread his hands in a graphic illustration of the way Karen had moulded them to her belly just a short time previously, and she saw that they were both trembling visibly. 'Our baby,' he finished with a determined nod.

'My stomach's full of butterflies, Sue,' Kara whispered. 'Why on earth did we let you and Mike talk us into this?'

'Because after all that you and Mac have been through, nothing less would do,' Sue said in her usual no-nonsense tone. 'Anyway, you're family and this is a family wedding.'

Kara shook her head at the crazy pace life had taken on in the last few months.

Mike had been quite right when he'd warned her that Mac still had a long way to go, but he'd forgotten to count on Mac's stubbornness and determination.

The trouble was, each time one of them had tried to talk him into slowing down a little he'd turned his dark eyes on them and reminded them of how much he'd already missed.

'I knew nothing about her until you were in labour,' he'd said as he'd carefully cradled Faith in his arms. 'I don't intend missing another minute if I don't have to.'

And then he'd set off again on another punishing round of exercises, both physical and mental, designed to hone his body and mind into something he could live with.

Kara had been glad to discover that he had no memory of the actual crash and, as Mike had repeatedly warned her, only brief flashes of things from his time in the coma.

One thing that had startled him had been his first glimpse of his face in a mirror.

'What's happened to me?' he exclaimed, drawing Kara to his side in a hurry.

'What's the matter?' she asked, her eyes anxiously travelling over him. She couldn't see anything wrong. He looked the same as he had for months, except now he was very wide awake.

'My face… And my hair!' He gestured at his reflection in the mirror. 'How long was I in that coma? Was it months or years? I've gone grey!'

Kara couldn't help chuckling a little. She'd grown so used to seeing him like that that she'd actually forgotten about the changes.

'It looks very distinguished,' she soothed as she smoothed the few silvery strands that had appeared at his temples during the course of his illness. 'I'm sure Faith will give you a lot more of those before she finally leaves home.'

'She's just been born. Don't talk about her leaving home,' he objected. 'Anyway,' he continued, sometimes struggling to find a word although he was recovering his former fluency with amazing speed, 'if you think I'm going to let any lecherous young men get close enough to propose marriage, you've got another think coming. Once she hits puberty I'm locking her up in her room.'

'The same way you locked *me* in your room?' she teased, and then smiled a secret smile when she saw his cheeks darken and his pupils begin to dilate. She was just so glad that their time together was still intact in his memory. It had been such a special magical time.

'What happened to my nose?' Mac demanded, dragging her away from her thoughts.

'You broke it,' she reminded him.

'Yes. I know. Playing rugby. But I ended up with a lump and a twist in it.'

'And then it was broken again in the crash and set properly, so you can count it as an unexpected bonus.' She paused and threw him a wicked grin. 'It seems to have stopped you snoring, too.'

'I don't snore!' he objected, instantly leaping to his own defence the way he had ever since the first time she'd teased him about it.

'Not any more,' she agreed. 'And you're more handsome than ever. Aren't I lucky?' She batted her eyelashes ferociously and made him laugh.

But she didn't feel like laughing now.

'What on earth made your parents offer to organise all this?' she demanded, as she waited for the organ music to start. She fiddled nervously with the bouquet of freesias Mac had arranged for her to carry. She'd been so surprised when she'd received them that she'd almost cried. He had absolutely no memories of their first wedding day and yet he had ordered an identical bouquet of flowers for her this time too.

'Mine and Mike's,' Sue reminded her. 'They said they'd worked so well together and enjoyed organising ours so much that they wanted to do it all over again. As they didn't have any more children of their own, willing to oblige them, they've adopted you and Mac.'

'Well, I hope they understand how much we appreciate it,' she said with a misty smile. 'The two of us would never have been able to have done this by ourselves in the time available, and we really wanted it to be today.'

It was exactly a year ago today that they should have married, and now, after a year filled with despair, desperation and just a miracle or two, it was finally going to happen.

The music began, and when she pictured Mac, waiting for her at the front of the tiny church, instantly all the butterflies vanished.

'Ready?' she asked Sue with a smile that suddenly grew a little wider when she heard Faith join in with the music.

Mac was sitting in his wheelchair as she approached up the short aisle, his new dark suit jacket fitting perfectly across the muscles he'd worked so hard to rebuild.

He'd tried to insist that he wouldn't need the despised chair today until Kara had suggested he might like to conserve his strength for other activities later in the day.

In the end they'd compromised, and as she drew to a halt beside him he stood up out of the chair and offered her his arm as Mike slid it out of the way.

'Darroch James MacGregor, do you take this woman…?' intoned the priest, his voice filling the flower-bedecked church.

'Kara Louise Desmond, do you take this man…?'

She turned her head to look up into Mac's eyes, his beautiful, dark, wickedly gleaming, happy eyes, and couldn't help smiling as her joy overflowed.

'I do,' she vowed from her heart.

'Kara, I'd like you to meet Ted Carrick,' Mac said soon after they'd arrived at the church hall for the reception.

Not wanting to test Mac's stamina, they'd opted not to have a formal reception line. This meant that for the past few minutes they'd been surrounded by a miniature whirlwind of people as they each took their turn to sit down with Mac and Kara for a few minutes' conversation.

At Mac's introduction, Kara turned and found herself looking into a smiling face with a pair of the most amazingly intent eyes.

'Hi, Kara,' he said in his instantly recognisable American accent. 'If I say I've heard a lot about you, it sounds like I'm using a line, but it's the truth.' He grasped her hand in both of his and squeezed it. 'I've been looking forward to thanking you for all the hard work you put in on this sorry specimen. I suppose there must have been some reason why you wanted to keep him...'

Kara chuckled, liking him instantly. 'Oh, if you've got a year or two to spare, I could tell you a few of them,' she retorted. 'Actually, I've been wanting to meet you so I could thank *you*. Without your knowledge...without your advice...' She shook her head, unable to continue, her throat closing up with emotion.

'But, Kara, without someone willing to put in the hours of dedication, all the knowledge in the world wouldn't have done Mac any good. If you put half the effort into your marriage that you put into his recovery, he's going to be a very happy man.'

'I intend to put in at least ten times the effort,' Kara declared, caught between tears and laughter as he pretended to mop his brow at the thought.

'I hope you mean that,' Mac whispered, as his mentor moved off to be introduced to Professor Squires by Mike.

'Mean what?' Kara was momentarily distracted by the sight of Sue's mother narrowly avoiding a tug of war with Mike's mother as each wanted to cuddle Faith.

'That you're going to put ten times the effort into our marriage, of course. Does that mean that I'll be able to lie back and enjoy myself?'

'Some of the time,' she agreed. 'But, then, if you want to find out what sort of underwear I've chosen to wear today, you might just want to put in a little effort of your own...'

'Witch!' he accused on a husky chuckle. 'Are you sure that sort of temptation is good for me?'

'I'm sure it is, but we can always find out tonight.'

'Mac!' exclaimed a voice as he pushed the door open. 'And Kara and the baby!'

Alison hurried towards them with a welcoming smile on her face. 'Oh, it's so good to see you all. Are you here for a visit?'

Before they could answer they were surrounded by people and voices, all just as welcoming.

'Haven't you got enough work to do?' Mike demanded as he joined the throng, but his complaint fell on deaf ears.

'When are you coming back to us?' That was Alison again, getting straight to the point. 'Mike said you were improving by leaps and bounds.'

'I've still got my limitations,' Mac warned.

'So has every man, but it doesn't stop them,' Alison retorted, to chuckles.

'True,' Mac agreed wryly. 'But in my case, they will affect the way I work.'

'In what way?' That was Gaynor.

'My night vision is very poor, and probably always will be,' he admitted. 'I tend to bump into things and trip over them.'

'So stay in bed. It won't matter if you bump into things there,' Alison muttered to Kara with a wink.

'And I've still got a stubborn residual weakness on my left side,' Mac continued, pretending to ignore the burst of giggles even though the heat in his cheeks told Kara he'd heard Alison's comment.

'Well, as the rest of us mere mortals were never as ambidextrous as you were, it probably puts us on a par at last,' Mike said, as he wrapped an arm briefly around his friend's shoulders. 'Seriously, Mac. The department will welcome you with open arms as soon as you feel you're ready to come back. Professor Squires and I are quite happy if you'd rather not do the neurosurgery any more—we both know you were always more interested in the other side anyway.'

Kara was watching Mac as Mike spoke, and saw the last of the tension leave him. He hadn't said much about this visit to his old haunts but she'd known he was worried about the shape the rest of his life was going to take.

'Do you want to see your old room?' Gaynor offered. 'We've been thinking of putting up a plaque in memory of the millennium miracle that happened in there.'

Mac shook his head and wrapped his arm around Kara, enclosing both her and their baby.

'It wasn't the room that made the miracle happen, it was this woman and this baby. Kara believed in me—she had faith enough for both of us that I'd eventually come out of it. But it was little Faith here that finally kick-started me—literally!'

'Come here, my love,' Mac whispered, and beckoned Kara from the other side of the room.

Kara paused with her hand twisted up behind her to reach for the tab of her zip.

'I was just going to get undressed.' She paused for a moment to allow her eyes to travel over him.

The bedside light was spilling over him, much as the light over his hospital bed had done, and the white sheet was drawn up to his waist, truncating that sexy broad arrow of dark silky hair that narrowed on its way over his flat abdomen.

The difference this time was the wicked glint the light was picking up in his eyes and the curve of his smile as he continued to beckon her over.

'Let me do the honours for you,' he offered. 'I really think I ought to give my nerves and muscles a bit of a workout—just to make certain that everything is kept up to peak performance.'

Kara chuckled at his nonsense, but as she willingly made her way towards him she could feel the start of her answering arousal.

'Far be it from me to prevent you from getting a good workout. After all, that's why I invested in such a variety of underwear—just to make certain you didn't get bored with your exercises…'

She was within reach now, and he grabbed her hand and tumbled her across his lap in a laughing heap.

'Kara, you could wear cast-iron underwear, no underwear or any variety in between, and it wouldn't make any difference. It's not the underwear that matters but the person wearing it...or not, as the case may be. It's *you* that's important—the most important person in my life. Without you I wouldn't *have* a life—literally. You're my own personal millennium miracle.'

Kara reached up to stroke his face, the precious, handsome face she'd so nearly lost, and counted her own blessings. She would never forget how close tragedy had come, but now was the time for celebrating life.

'Speaking of miracles,' she said, with an experimental wriggle on his lap that told her what she wanted to know, 'I think you've managed one of your own. How about—?'

She never got to finish the question as he bent his head and kissed her into silence.

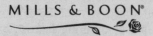

MILLS & BOON®

Makes
any time
special

Enjoy a romantic novel from
Mills & Boon®

Presents...™ *Enchanted*™ TEMPTATION®

Historical Romance™ ✚MEDICAL
ROMANCE™

MILLS & BOON®

MEDICAL ROMANCE™

GOOD HUSBAND MATERIAL by Sheila Danton

Rebecca Groom soon realises how attractive she finds the senior partner, Dr Marc Johnson. But the surgery intends to expand, using an old house that holds dear memories for Rebecca...

ALWAYS MY VALENTINE by Leah Martyn

Charge Nurse Geena Wilde liked Dr Jack O'Neal very much, but it wasn't until Valentine's Day that Geena received a gorgeous bunch of red roses from Jack, and an invitation to the Valentine Ball! That was a *very* good beginning...

COURTING DR CADE by Josie Metcalfe

Damon and Katherine were instant friends. Now Katherine's grandmother will lose her beloved home unless Katherine is married by Leap Year's day! But a simple marriage of convenience turns into something far more complicated!

A FAMILY CONCERN by Margaret O'Neill

For Gemma Fellows and her six-year-old daughter, Daisy, the cottage is a godsend. It's a new start—and as far as Dr Sam Mallory is concerned, Gemma and Daisy are perfect for him...

Available from 4th February 2000

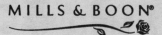

MILLS & BOON®

Makes any time special™

Bestselling themed romances brought back to you by popular demand

Each month By Request brings you three full-length novels in one beautiful volume featuring the best of the best.

So if you missed a favourite Romance the first time around, here is your chance to relive the magic from some of our most popular authors.

Look out for

Kids &
Kisses

in January 2000

featuring Lucy Gordon, Rebecca Winters and Emma Goldrick

4 FREE

books and a surprise gift!

We would like to take this opportunity to thank you for reading this Mills & Boon® book by offering you the chance to take FOUR more specially selected titles from the Medical Romance™ series absolutely FREE! We're also making this offer to introduce you to the benefits of the Reader Service™—

★ FREE home delivery
★ FREE gifts and competitions
★ FREE monthly Newsletter
★ Exclusive Reader Service discounts
★ Books available before they're in the shops

Accepting these FREE books and gift places you under no obligation to buy, you may cancel at any time, even after receiving your free shipment. Simply complete your details below and return the entire page to the address below. *You don't even need a stamp!*

YES! Please send me 4 free Medical Romance books and a surprise gift. I understand that unless you hear from me, I will receive 6 superb new titles every month for just £2.40 each, postage and packing free. I am under no obligation to purchase any books and may cancel my subscription at any time. The free books and gift will be mine to keep in any case.

M0EA

Ms/Mrs/Miss/Mr ....Initials.................................
BLOCK CAPITALS PLEASE

Surname ....

Address ....

....

....Postcode.................................

Send this whole page to:
UK: FREEPOST CN81, Croydon, CR9 3WZ
EIRE: PO Box 4546, Kilcock, County Kildare (stamp required)

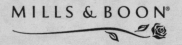

MILLS & BOON®

Coming in January 2000...

ACCIDENT AND
EMERGENCY

Three exciting stories based in the casualty departments of busy hospitals. Meet the staff who juggle an active career and still find time for romance and the patients who depend on their care to reach a full recovery.

Three of your favourite authors:

Caroline Anderson

Josie Metcalfe

Sharon Kendrick